Tellin

Sophie Marceau became an actress at the age of thirteen. She has since starred in some of the major box office successes of recent years, including *Braveheart* and *The World is Not Enough*. *Telling Lies* is her first novel. She lives in Paris with her husband Andrzej Zulawski and their son.

Telling Lies

Sophie Marceau

Translated by
Adriana Hunter

PHŒNIX

A PHOENIX PAPERBACK ORIGINAL

First published in France in 1996 by Editions Stock
This edition first published in Great Britain in 2001 by Phoenix,
a division of Orion Books Ltd,
Orion House, 5 Upper Saint Martin's Lane
London, WC2H 9EA

A CIP catalogue record for this book is available
from the British Library.

ISBN 0753 814315

Typeset at The Spartan Press Ltd, Lymington, Hants
Printed by Clays Ltd, St Ives plc

1

This is another life. When I wake, the newness of the day wraps itself around me and, with a barely whispered breath in my ear, caresses me with its veil of light. Everything else is just memories. All jumbled up. What was yesterday is now confused with a more distant past, what was true with what was false. The dust from the theatre has disappeared as a dream does on waking, fleeing in the face of hard reality. The smell of warm bread rises up to the second floor and insinuates itself through the half-open window of my bedroom. I'd forgotten, some time ago, that there was a bakery on the ground floor of the building – and people coming to buy their bread.

Today is not like other days. For some time now I've been walking a tightrope with no sign of a safety net. I've escaped into the security of routine, standing fair and square on its two feet, unimaginative and endless, as calm as a house in the country. Now the routine is becoming abstract and is changing. It's waiting to see where it should land, where to find a new home. It's becoming loneliness – a loneliness lost in the time it takes to breathe that final 'ess' for infinity.

I am weightless now, afraid of disappearing, of being intoxicated by so much space. How am I going to absorb all of this and make use of it as if it were some revitalising force? How am I going to avoid breaking apart, being torn up into shreds and scattering, dispersing into a million stars? Temptation in the shape of a free woman – a strange and evil attraction. I hear the sirens' song inviting me to discover everything that is beautiful and vast. I know they want to tear me apart. I can see their victims' pallid blood streaming behind the skin of their faces. I am tempted to send all of this to the devil, but I immediately regret using his name, knowing that he is listening, he is waiting, somewhere in the heart of me, ready to bite the flesh. Is he answerable for my weaknesses, my spinelessness? Is he hiding the truth from me? Will it be through his eyes that I see the world?

He left this morning, taking only a few books in a big, shapeless bag. He went down the crooked staircase.

No one walks better than he does. His feet perfectly straight. I would have liked to feel his hand slapping me, making the air moan. But he was untouchable, hardened from head to foot by a fatal cramp. The mercury dispersed its venom. Rigid and dead, he went down the crooked staircase.

Maybe there never was a smell of warm bread, nor any people in the bakery that morning. It is Sunday, inevitably Sunday, recognisable even with your nose buried under the sheets. I can hear the bells and I can imagine the golden sheen of the warm croissants on a large tray, dogs, children, toy balls that narrowly miss toppling the scald-ing tea, stockinged feet like in the instant coffee ads, Sunday as it is on the television. A long, snaking draught intrudes its way to me; the living room still smells of cigarettes, is still littered with coats and sweaters, dirty upturned shoes, the leftovers of a sparse improvised supper, bathed in the haze of the ash-blue morning, tepid as the skin of a corpse stagnating in its indifference, caricaturing its own last expression, leaving things as they are. The tiled floor of the kitchen is ice cold. The telephone wire is curled up on itself, liked twisted pasta.

Completely naked, or nearly, I remember a headache and I stay rooted to the spot, not knowing where to start, whether to put on a pair of socks which will get dirty the minute they touch the floor, to put the water on to boil for a cup of tea, or to leave straight away, and take stock of my unhappiness in the street amongst the passers-by with their neat hair, their Sunday clothes and their happy faces. There are knots in my hair, I flatten them as I have seen drunken men do with the flat of their greasy hands.

I burrow my fists into the depths of my pockets to pull my trousers below my waist, shifting them down from their original position and dragging the concertinaed folds of the trouser legs in the dust, rasping the hem along the tarmac. The seat of the trousers hangs down, flattening the outline into a cubist shape, and with the sway of each step the fabric is sheared by the join between the buttocks and the tops of the thighs. My heavy boots emerge from the bottom of the trousers like great boulders, looking like badly drawn feet. I catch sight of myself in the shop windows. Putting the background out of focus, my eyes delight in pulling focus backwards and forwards like the perfect lens of a camera, and I'm happy to be dirty and dishevelled out in the street. I won't go very far, I know I'm near the apartment, and I quickly turn left down the next street, which completes the one-block loop of my expedition. With my tummy exposed and flat from not having eaten, hard as hunger itself, I make fun of everyone by showing

3

that you can make fun of yourself, let yourself go, that the body is nothing, nor is hunger or femininity. I want them to know that I have something else to worry about.

I worry about emptiness, but I am so involved in worrying about emptiness that I forget how cold it is, and I deliberately flatten my dirty hair across my head like a bandage. I want people to think I'm ill. I want them to feel sorry for me. I cling to the image I see of myself in the shop windows, just to be sure that someone at least is looking at me, to be sure that I exist. Feeling hunger gnawing at me with its little bribery to stay alive, I fracture myself into the contradiction: to be, not to be. I would like to hold out without eating and to lose weight visibly as I yearn for purification and a fresh start.

No one has noticed me. I tried to advertise my loneliness but it is as if no one believed in it, expecting me to be greedy and strong, to have steady feet slender enough to fit into pretty narrow little shoes, to wear figure-hugging clothes, to hold my head high and turn heads.

It was a failed attempt. I'm devastated to see myself like this as I walk the last side of the block heading for the corner, where the door to my apartment building is hidden behind the shop-front of the bakery . . . which is closed today.

I'm hungry.

'He' could be called Julian, Matthew, John, he could have different faces, it could just as easily be today as a long time ago, in another life, he could be a stranger – especially a stranger, from somewhere else, who speaks a language that I understand. He could be or might no longer be, it doesn't matter to me, it's him, just him.

*

4

I don't tell the truth because I like mystery, the things that people don't say. I am only happy with my own silence, in the room where my secrets belong. That is where I play on my own, disorganised, nasty if I want to be, manipulative, in love – and even intelligent. I dilute my story with hazy detail, scattering it here and there, mixing and jumbling the petty order of our lives. Because I don't believe in beginnings and ends, because chance doesn't exist, and chaos obeys rules that are not rules at all, because time does the same, because I don't want anything. So I take skeletons to pieces bone by bone, I don't invent anything that isn't already there. Let me be mad and sincere in my own way; the only pretension I have is in my heart. This is one story that I won't be telling because it's just another story like millions of others. Everything is a story, every second of a life tells a story, but what will death remember? Do we have to live these stories or can we forget them and keep just the grit and the scum of the days accumulated in us? None of us knows why we are as we are. Why do we love? or want? Why do we stop loving? Why do we feel lonely? Why do we want to do wrong, either something petty or something terrible? I take comfort from a Zen text: *Wonder of wonders. All living creatures are intrinsically Bud-dhas, blessed with wisdom and virtue, but they do not know it because men's spirits have been corrupted by deceitful thoughts.*

And me, what could happen to me? Every day I think it's going to be like this for ever. So I feel bored and moody. I'm often in a bad mood even if no one can actually say that they have seen me 'sour-faced' – I like seducing them too much to disappoint them and show them a mask of bitterness. In truth, I'm even sad, always sad. If I knew how to sing, I'd sing the blues with a down-turned mouth and huge great tears, I would be thin and would smoke

5

cigarettes, I'd drink white wine, champagne or vodka ostentatiously, and I'd drag myself around complaining about the whole world, sinking drunkenly into a spiral of unhappiness.

But life has decided otherwise. I look about fifteen, I sometimes carry a little too much weight, I've given up smoking, I go to bed early and I prefer red wine to anything else. And I still don't know whether or not that, too, is a lie. Surely a choice automatically implies a half-measure, and therefore a half-happiness, and eventually – from time to time, out of the blue – a longing for what was lost? And then everything changes again. It was meant to be for life, those days of good resolutions, of growing up wise and reasonable with a sense of History. History, I could already see myself inscribed in it for exemplary behaviour, as an exception to the rule. Now, that's the perfect couple, they would have said, upright, good-looking, no complications or dirty secrets. I wasn't completely happy because I wasn't completely in on it, sufficiently in on it not to look at the outside world, not to want to show what I was capable of. Torn between love – the real love – and the portrayal I made of it. Because I'm guilty of being what I am: a child like every other child who believes everything that good Christian thinking has taught them – that they are sinful creatures, responsible for the suffering of others, doomed to repentance. And so I lie, for fear of divine retribution, or rather for fear of how I am judged collectively; I put on a brave face, I'm clean and well-behaved, I wash clean my sins every evening like a little pair of knickers, and I never think of Evil. I have no fantasies, I give money to the poor and I'm as naïve as a flower surrounded by millions of other flowers in a green meadow that smells of springtime.

What is the point of that, apart from self-deception? Why lie to yourself like that just to end up thinking of yourself as a monster capable of the worst, ready to betray everything? Because you hate yourself, and – given that you hate yourself – you can do Evil. I have done it. Not to some moral standard but to a man made of flesh and feelings, a strong free man who fought against all perverted forms of power, striking out on his own and threatened by the thunderbolts of outraged gods who punished his audacity for reaching such heights.

I wanted to touch the butterfly's wing; I nearly broke it. I had to feel how fragile it was. To feel, with the tip of my finger, the downy surface palpitating feverishly, seeping so much that it dissolved, stuck to the moist skin of my assassin's finger. I held my breath, so that my blood no longer flowed for as long as it took the miracle to happen, that little energy of life-force flowing from the tips of the fingers and penetrating the damaged tissues of the sleeping butterfly's wing.

The big table, as long as the one at which Jesus sat with the apostles, is scattered with things, with vases and books. Some of them have already been started and are resting nose-down on the wood. Others, still closed, are piled up, thick and shiny. I prefer to read in the morning, but I rarely take the time to sit down and turn the pages. As if the morning were intended for something other than reading, as if at this time of day man was programmed to get up and go out to work.

In my family, they have lived like this for ever, and they think of reading and thinking as wasted time. They stamp holes in their time noisily as if it were a train ticket, endlessly repeating the same gestures, doing and undoing

– what a lot of work a house takes – and for a whole lifetime they keep going back over the same housework with the earnestness of those who believe they never had any choice. With a conviction that they are doing better and being more useful than those who sit idly while they come and go industriously, they fuss and sweat over the washing-up, wanting it spotless, finished, tidied away. Without the housework and the shopping to do they'd probably be bored, and they do a maximum of work so that the maximum time passes without their being constrained to stop and look at themselves, and they talk to avoid the silence that makes them profoundly uncomfortable, like a strong liquor which threads its way down the throat and burns the chest. They complain of always having too much to do, in fact they are complaining of having enslaved themselves to their own boredom. So they blame life for being like this, for denying them any personal choice, they call themselves victims of a superior force which mistreats them, and they submit to the mortal rules of their system of repetition.

This morning I could, therefore, resort to getting on with the housework and sweating over getting the apartment clean. I choose this solution, finding it reassuring to have so many things to do. The morning will go more quickly then. Knowing that I have taken the easy option, I clean the apartment from top to bottom, as good a little housewife as I have been taught to be. I can admire my work and put off till tomorrow what can wait: those abandoned books which make no demands on anyone, as opposed to the great piles of dirty washing-up, condemned – whichever way you looked at it – to be in great piles and dirty. At last it's done and I too am clean and tidy, and sweet-smelling. It's nearly midday.

I finally sit down for a couple of hours, in my clean apartment, clean too myself. I open my book and this constant struggle against time disappears while I read. The world is revealed to us by books, not by housework. The inexplicable becomes familiar, God appears in the shape of an interrogation, admitted without a reply. Sunday flows into the afternoon and the light changes, tarnished like a girl's skin which, though she could still be called young, no longer has the glowing, mocking effrontery of a virgin's. The light dulls and sends a veil of shadows sliding over the skin. The brightness imperceptibly leaks out its brilliance before disappearing. I think of Juliet . . .

Come, night! come, Romeo! come, thou day in night!
For thou wilt lie upon the wings of night,
Whiter than new snow on a raven's back.
Come, gentle night; come, loving, black-brow'd night,
Give me my Romeo: and, when he shall die,
Take him and cut him out in little stars,
And he will make the face of heaven so fine
That all the world will be in love with night,
And pay no worship to the garish sun.

I deliberately go back along the corridor to look again at *Rhapsodie du spectre comme si brûlait la dernière nuit*. But the corridor is too tall and narrow, I have to crane my neck to see it. The painting is not as beautiful as it was, and I'm disappointed at having come to see it. And I discover what I already know: I must leave.

My new apartment is in a chic, expensive street. A pretty little square box, in shiny white paper – stupid, really.

We – that is my apartment and I – have a purely

functional relationship. It will never do anything to surprise me, it is set within its four walls. Only at night do the spaces become more fluid, but I don't like the night, and I sleep.

We used to meet three mornings a week. He would arrive, fresh and uncomplicated. I would have just woken up, curled in my little square, my legs heavy, my body needing oxygen. I could tell that he soon felt awkward, he couldn't wait to escape and breathe the outside air under the little squares of blue sky. I was happy to follow him – I would have followed him anywhere. His warm gentle hand was the first sign of life in this whole expanse of indolence. In his hand, I had the heart of a child again. I imagined the sun, the water, I transformed myself into a great balloon. My eyes widened, I had become weightless again. He didn't change. He didn't let go of my hand. He could always sense that little something, something rather like fear.

I used to get ideas into my head, to arrange the world to suit me, and I'd invent a character for myself to play. I was the heroine of an American film. Crushing the swarming world underfoot, I'd take out my weapon and shoot the baddies. I'd die, leaving desolation behind me. Fiction was becoming reality, I was carrying on on my way without looking left or right. And I saw him. There was a man there, next to me, his body somehow deranged. He couldn't see me, his eyes were distant, reddened with horror and exhaustion. As if a hand had come up out of the ground and grabbed me by the neck to lower my head and force me to understand the one thing there was to understand, I looked at his feet. It was then that I felt my heart breaking, and where it was broken the nerve of Evil, the truth of this world, could be seen beating. This man had been emptied, sucked dry, he no longer had anything of himself. He no longer had any shoes.

I felt that fragility. Under my finger, the demented palpitations of the butterfly's wing.

It was with that same finger that I remember touching a child's hand for the first time, letting my index finger slide into the chubby palm, so soft that my finger was surprised at the touch of it. Communication from another world is still suspended in that hand, like a sign, a forerunner of our lost writings that are found in the middle of nowhere in some desolate abandoned place where a few unknown creatures still draw breath. That hand connected me to my world, to my origins. It told me that it knew me and all sorts of stories came back to me, and told me that I might not be living for nothing.

2

Someone had put their hand on my shoulder, like a dove bearing news. It was the hand of a tall woman, a woman I knew and recognised immediately, and she woke me from my melancholy torpor. My body was warm and snug, my face pale. I could see that she was flushed with excitement with a little froth of saliva in the corners of her mouth. Her hair was tightly curled like someone who had just left the hairdresser. She came from the far end of the room, out of breath, tall and thin but gentle and reassuring. She came straight out and told me that he wanted to meet me, this evening, straight away, that he was on his way. The plot had been thickening without my even realising it. She had come to wake me, reaching out her hand to me as if she knew how difficult things had been, as if she knew . . .

'He wants you for his next film . . .'

I lived in Nice at the time, where the pebble beach is, above the Croisette, where the road curves round, in a little hotel sheltered behind a solid mass of rock graciously draped in trees. I could hear the sea, just by pushing open the window. I could also hear the bustle and fanfares of the Cannes Film Festival in the distance. At the time, I was in rehearsal for *The Taming of the Shrew* at the Théâtre de la

Ville in Nice. I was meekly meeting the needs of an egocentric actor who was perfectly devoid of that brand of sex appeal that only film actors have to have, and I filled my own feelings of emptiness by being a stooge to him, the man, the hero the ac-tor. But it was Shakespeare that I wanted to serve, so I didn't pay much attention to my partner's stage directions.

Some friends came to invite me to the screening of a film that very evening in the Grand Palais du Festival. I was wearing my gum-boots. I'd just come back from a walk on the beach and they'd seemed the obvious solution to avoid hurting myself walking on the pebbles: walking with my boots on in the water where the bottom was sandy. My cheeks must have been red, and my nose too, my face fresh and firm. Cannes seemed to be swarming with people and somehow false, over made-up. I still had no make-up on, and I bought a black straw hat to cover up my lank hair; I found a light polka-dot dress and, with my legs firmed up by the sea and the exercise, I slipped on a pair of sandals that buckled up round the ankles and added a good three inches to my height.

When I looked at him for the first time it was as I would still look at him twelve years later, with a mixture of confidence and amazement. And yet, I didn't know him.

He sat down in the middle of the auditorium, attracting the ebb and flow of unstable energies that teemed round the great padded space. His film was about to scorch itself onto the screen and onto the blind eyes of his audience. He bit his lips in anticipation. I recognised them, him and his cast – no one could fail to recognise the actress who had the place of honour that evening.

She's shorter than you think, and slimmer – the screen

14

puts on the pounds. Her outfit is not flamboyant; she looks worried. The strands of her big black boa looping into the small of her back keep quivering and slipping from her athletic white shoulders. I was in the middle of it, submerged in waves of dinner jackets, right there in the best seats, where the guests sit.

I must have seen him sit down and, even though I don't remember it, I now imagine that he ran his hand through his hair as he always does. His hands looked sharp, pointed, as they emerged from the sleeves of his dinner jacket, and all his nervous energy was concentrated in his wide shoulders propping up the unseasonably warm jacket. I could sense the irregular palpitations of his heart, guess the taut expression on his face which was pale as a prisoner's on the first day of release. It mattered to him to be there.

Before the lights even came back up the applause could already be heard. People broke into unrestrained whooping and cheering. I smiled, happy that others were shouting for me. I remember him then, standing, turned towards me, waving to the audience. He didn't see me.

There was a moment of suspension, a last breath before leaping into the void. A pause which allowed for the grace of God – and for that sharp intake of breath on the brink of the hiatus. And I went back to my little castle nestled on its rock just above the turn in the road to pack my scruffy, broken bag. Floundering in the sinking, shifting sands, I struggled to build up the rickety scaffolding of my new life.

I had lovers, several at a time. A married man who'd waited until his wife had left with their two children, who'd also waited for me to grow up, because the first time we'd worked together I was only thirteen. I met him a few years

15

later, he'd not forgotten me. He'd been counting the days, and the evening after his beloved left he was in my bed.

I liked him, he liked sex. He told me about his wife; said that she still wore size eight trousers and that she'd managed to stay slim after her pregnancies. He kept saying that during the last weekend we'd all spent together by the first assistant director's pool, he'd seen us swimming side by side and it had excited him. I didn't think that was right but I'd been drifting idly through life for a while by then. Boredom had made me stupid, it meant that I was attracted by anything anyone said or did, by sleeping, smoking, drinking. Life flowed over me like the men and the alcohol which made me sad and exuberant by turns.

It didn't last more than a few months one spring. I soon gave the elbow to one of them, the most devoted one perhaps, the first. I kept the second, the official clandestine lover. The third one had disgusted me straight away. He only had me once, and afterwards I sat for hours and hours on a bank of fresh grass, feeling soiled and wanting to be sick. I wanted to cut myself into tiny pieces, not to be myself any more, to make everything that had touched me disappear: his hands, his erection, the memory of him; to melt into lead and burn the impurities.

That year a film-producer friend and I had managed to get two rooms at the Hotel Majestic in Cannes at the last minute. One of them was small and not too pricey – a sort of overflow room. The other had just become available, it was a big expensive suite. He found the whole thing very amusing, saying there was some symbolic meaning in it and, in a rush of generosity, he offered me the suite fit for a star. I spent one night in it.

It was the last night of the old white Palais. I too was

dressed in white, an elegant backless catsuit in white satin which hugged my neck in a little stand-up collar. I walked along the red carpet, I was a tall girl, and I was noticed by the crowd and the festival-goers. In the morning, I dived into the hotel's deserted swimming-pool. I went back across the lobby still wet, scantily covered by my bath towel, barefoot on the grey carpet which soaked up the water trickling from my swimming costume and my soaking wet hair. The air was so warm that I'd forgotten to dry myself. I slipped between the soberly dressed maîtres d'hôtel towards the lifts. In the constricted space of the lift I curled up my naked toes surrounded by hard and threatening shoes, I wrapped myself modestly in my damp towel, and made myself as small as possible between twin men dressed in identical dinner jackets, they were tired and smelled of cigar smoke and peppery after-shave. I was going up to change, they were coming home to bed.

It was the same producer friend who introduced us. The three of us were sitting on the hotel terrace, I don't remember why. He'd seen me in the swimming-pool, I was looking at something else, I was young. He'd started thinking dreamily about something, he told me later, but he doesn't remember exactly what: the way a whole lifetime can skip by in just one second, or something like that.

'Like a dove bearing news.'

This long, firm hand was like a friend. It gently brushed my shoulder with the wholesome energy of an angel, stroking and purifying the skin with a single touch. I felt somehow guilty and I wanted to cry, I felt like a little girl again, sad and pretty as a doll crying because she's inadvertently crushed a snail under a leaf on the wet path. The sound of the shell breaking, the feel of it giving

17

way under her foot, and it's too late, the animal's dead, the shell is shattered into tiny pieces, the mystery of these mineral pieces and this life that cannot be put back together.

When he went down the stairs, I felt no more grown-up and I still wanted to cry.

He came right up to me. How did he know? Fighting against the current of my life, he back-tracked his way to me, a solitary figure battling against the grain of the giant swishing hairs along a dog's back, wild and pure, following his unadulterated male instinct. He came to find me. He approached me politely, like the prince in a fairy tale under the blossoming linden tree. I sat at the heavy wrought iron table, my elbows forming a V on its curving, circular designs, and I listened to him speak, caught out by his perceptiveness. He told me about his film, that was all, and I felt that I had found my twin. I didn't try to understand it, it just felt right. I knew that he would protect me.

> For Love . . . has two faces; one white, the other black; two bodies; one smooth, the other hairy. It has two hands, two feet, two nails, two, indeed, of every member and each one is the exact opposite of the other.

Virginia Woolf was intrigued by love, but I was discovering it.

And yet it is men who are afraid of women. Are we covered in hair? Where are we hiding our tails? Behind us! Saul Bellow says that women eat lettuce and drink human blood, and there all those others too who describe us as evil creatures – the Bible, for a start. If I stop to think, I can even frighten myself. I've had those looks, intrigued but wary, not sure whether to succumb or to flee. I've tried to reassure, to explain, I've even sworn to something I wasn't sure of myself – that I'm incapable of betrayal. I still believe this: men judge by actions, women by faith. We cannot see the madness, it is within us, like the hysteria in our bellies. We believe ourselves to be ugly when we are all the prettier for being gentle and unaffected, and we believe ourselves to be beautiful when we are sure of ourselves, and therefore just a mite vulgar, or even common.

We are the common people, we are the earth. We live underground and eat the earth, we are dark, fertile, heavy. Their feet get clogged, bogged down, and we don't move. Film stars, real film stars, are only really stars when they don't yet know it. Dietrich in *Blue Angel*, Marilyn appearing short and plump as she managed – or not – to stay until her death. And Garbo quite unaccountable, unique, androgynous, defying all the usual rules about women, and too beautiful for any man. The traces of some imminent femininity were already there to see on Orlando's face.

Over the obscure man is poured the merciful suffusion of darkness.

Was it that that reassured me? Sensing a platinum twinkle troubling the sleek outline of his eye, coyly surrounded by fine black lashes. The sloping temples above the high white bone, questioning himself as a man in all his affirmation, as a man who is still actually a little boy marking this as an unresolved point in his life, as a man rendered fragile by his mother's absences and her sorcery, by a murderous female war which nurtured him as its own child, protecting him with its bombs – a monstrous mother who coupled with the Devil before this solitary, betrayed orphan.

He knows about lives quite different to his own, he has strange hands. His shapely masculine head brings to mind an octopus, such an intelligent animal that is neither male nor female, an animal which never seems to miss a thing.

I am instantly seduced by this great flesh of feelings, this enthralling complexity. I unfurl my wings and give free flow to the juices too long held back by paternal hands trying to protect me from being too much of a woman. I feel like a woman now, I feel myself returning to my state as earth, mystery, gentleness and protection. He will also be my defender, the caress on my cheek, he will always and forever be that endearing and self-contradictory look, the look of a man who is afraid but who loves all the same.

We left hand in hand, we told each other about ourselves and drank a great deal of wine. I laughed, it was so good. I didn't ask myself whether I was in love, it seemed like something other than love to me. It was better, bigger. Unnameable.

3

Digging back through the past when you're not really sure what's going on in the present. To find some sort of answer there, a sequence, a similarity. I've already told him the story of my life a thousand times; he knows that if I start again, it means something must be wrong.

We had to push the coffee table back to make room for the sofa-bed. The mechanical skeleton eased open, releasing the thin cramped mattress and spewing out crumpled sheets and a bolster which – rather cleverly – served as a pillow. That was where my parents slept, practically on the floor, only to get up to go to work as soon as dawn broke. The far side of the wall behind the sofa was our room, my brother's and mine. Beams protruded about half-way across the room, making an isosceles triangle. On one side was my brother's big bed and on the other the little bed that had always been mine. We often had friends to stay the night, and they managed to find room enough on the floor to arrange comfortable beds out of the sofa cushions which weren't needed at night. We would talk for hours, happy to be together. That was when we were fifteen.

For some of us life had got off to a bad start but we didn't ask them why, they only told us what they wanted to tell. One of them, a boy a little older than us, had spent a couple of nights with us and then my father said he couldn't come again. He'd sniffed him out as one crook might recognise another, or one man might be wary of another. We weren't allowed to see him. But away from home, in the afternoons when my parents were working, we saw a lot of him. Then he would disappear without any explanation, leaving no address, no family. We all thought that he lived alone and was cared for by Social Services or something like that. And yet he would produce wadges of big banknotes when we were clubbing together to pay the bill in the Italian restaurant where we met every Saturday evening. There were six of us, six friends. The same number of girls and boys, a permanently evolving mixture of brothers and sisters, friends, boyfriends and girlfriends. The sixth – who was in fact the fifth oldest – was the most nervous: I, who was the youngest, used to reassure him. The newcomer made seven.

That night we slept in our friends' parents' apartment because they'd gone away for two days. The seventh member and I kissed all night. Our eyes stinging in the dark, we could barely make each other out as the night gradually spun its cloak of sadness. In the weariness of the morning we each woke from our torpor. I enjoyed his kisses, enjoyed being stroked by his budding blond beard, fairer than the first light of dawn.

As night fell that evening he suddenly appeared outside my house, emerging from a doorway, a turning, ashen faced and with a knowing twinkle in his eye: he wanted to kiss me again. I wanted to run away this time but he held me in his strong freckled arms, stroking my back, so gently. I gave in. But I didn't love him, I didn't like the way he appeared from nowhere and lied without even saying anything. His little eyes were ringed with heavy shadows.

The entrance to the Châtelet metro station was right in front of us, vast, orange, round as a circus ring. Jostled and distorted by the crowd our seven-headed figure flowed and changed shape like the outline of an elastic band stretched on a little girl's playful fingers. There were policemen scattered here and there with their colts in their belts, and their caps clamped to their heads, shading their watchful eyes. It was as if something had exploded in the middle of the group: he shattered the outline of the circle and vanished into the teeming mass. His legs scissored back and forth as he slid obliquely away from us, cutting the ergonomic space of the crowd. In one stroke, one swift incision, he was gone. What we had all obscurely sensed had happened. Just before he escaped from view we saw him stop once and the suspicion of some emotion was etched on his face. He had paled. A white sweat trickled from his temples – he was afraid. And we left him to blend with the ever-changing dance of the elastic band.

We thought we would never see him again, or at least not for a long time. In the roasting red hell of Châtelet we were in collusion, the six of us once more.

There were two more stops to go before we got off.

He was waiting for us at the top of the steps, his hands thrust deep into the pockets of his bomber-jacket, his hair glowing gold in the wind, like a strange kind of angel. It was like a punishment seeing him there. I was afraid of him – I was always afraid when he appeared from nowhere like that. Made taller by the perspective of the staircase and given a shining aura by the light behind him, he towered over us, dominating us in his glory; but he was out of breath, the myth had been shattered and was living its final hours. One step after another, we climbed up the stark grey staircase and the angel shrank, returned to its human scale in its most banal form: he was little and a liar. His face oozed satisfaction. He took a revolver the size of a bottle of milk out of his jacket: none of us tried to take it or even touch it. He pressed it to his chest and put it back into his inside pocket.

The two sisters, as different from each other as a blond and a brunette could be, grew up. Our friend Jack went off with a different girlfriend. And the sixth member took to smoking cigarettes doused with trichloroethylene, tried to get work making porn films and then became a fishmonger.

Camus said: 'What reason is there for a man without a future to feel any emotion? That impassivity, that greatness in a man who has no hope, that eternal present – it is precisely this that enlightened theologians have called "hell".'

When I was eleven I flew in an aeroplane for the first time. I was tall and willowy, I wore my new sandals with the platform heels, I was conscious of my own maturity – I looked about sixteen. I haven't always been as pretty as I was that day.

I had my hair cut like a boy's, smoked long cigarettes, wore jeans and walked with a slouched back and bandy legs like a cowboy. My boyfriends loved me for ever. I loved them rather less. My parents, who'd been separated for two years, worked all the time. I stayed at home alone and did nothing, expected nothing and didn't resent the fact that time passed so slowly. I felt a whispering breath of life somewhere above my head, like a chick waiting for the shell to crack and for life to come and get it. I was ready.

I left home to live on my own when I was seventeen, in a little studio under the eaves. It was light and clean and even quite pretty, but I didn't like it, and I didn't like the area it was in either. I was working for an advertising agency and I was the little darling of all the Japanese and Koreans. With my Asian eyes and my dark complexion, I was a girl in full bloom, like the blossom of a Japanese cherry tree. *Kawai* (pretty)! I had money, enough. Occasionally I would go and help my parents, who'd recently got back together again, for a few hours a day. I would lay the tables, waitress for the midday meal and then help my mother sort out the kitchen. Sometimes I would stay and eat with my father, sitting up at the bar in their little brasserie. I was very fond of them.

Life went on.

If I move house, change my surroundings, I change my friends too. I've never learned to like the relations between friends. I prefer the relations between lovers, they seem more natural to me. I think of seduction as a sign of my interest in the other. It represents an exchange between 'I give' and 'I take'.

That's why I was so alone while I waited for the Other, for my fulfilment. Loneliness is a state of contemplation, a burning silence, and those moments mean everything to me. I was growing up, I was nearly eighteen.

I was impressed, affected by my new friends. They were different, more demanding. They appeared from nowhere and launched into my life. I was disorientated by their youthfulness, their freedom. With them the world opened up like a handkerchief which has been folded in a pocket. We held it in the palms of our hands, we were young.

When we got together it was to talk. One of them was called Marcel. His father was an immigrant from Algeria and his grandmother only spoke to him in Arabic. He was born in the south-west of France which tinted his Kabyle blue eyes with a hint of sun, water, girls and cicadas. He was a little overweight, or at least seemed to me to be. Either way, he was nice and even good-looking on occasions.

I'd met Marcel in my parents' café. He lived in a little room perched in the same building, six floors up. He came down to see us three or four times a day, to use the bathroom and to chat. When the sun was shining he would stay a little longer before going back up, his head full of ideas, to get back to his writing.

I never knew whether he found me attractive and I don't think he ever knew how I felt about him either. He had everything to do and I had everything to learn, our different fates automatically separated us, that's why our interest in each other never waned.

I liked the boys I knew: the louts, the sons of Communist workers, the young poets who would end up working in offices and the good-for-nothing boys on the street. I didn't like rich kids because they were rich, and everything else that went with it.

The first time it was a jeweller. He gave Mum a gold pendant. His shop was on the corner of the main shopping street in Courbevoie, and he had an apartment above the shop. He was the apple of his mother's eye, because he was the youngest and because his shop window was full of gold. He never opened the windows and we would spend long weekends together over that corner shop above the crossroads.

I got used to thinking that life was just like that. Later, there would be the children's bedroom. And then later, after that . . . nothing, I left. Quite within my rights, unchanged, but if you looked a little closer you could see the droop in the corners of my mouth, the glow of youthful grace fading. The veiled sparkle of a sad young girl.

I made love too young. I hardly dared look at the fragile body which swelled and furrowed mysteriously before me, still not understanding the currents that flowed within it, before it was violated by a curious outsider.

Watching shamelessly while you're tossed around and fumbled like a piece of luggage, allowing yourself to be squeezed by surly great hands which dominate your flesh, which deliberately mistreat it for the sake of their own pleasure. Desire is like submission; you have to humiliate or be humiliated, abandon all your good manners and any respect you might have had for the other, to sweat, pant, groan and open yourself up. Pleasure is dirty. Grown-ups aren't afraid of debasing themselves – they're ugly enough, anyway.

The first time, I didn't say anything. I saw myself completely naked, alone in the bathroom. I was bleeding. I didn't say anything to my mother, to anyone. It was my fault, it wasn't very pretty but everyone had to grow up. No one said anything to me either, and I accepted the betrayal. Ready to be used again, that was how I felt. Screwing myself up so that my breasts fell forward and my tummy creased, I looked at the place where you can see nothing and noticed, as I had noticed in my mother whom

I frequently saw naked, that the point of my pubis burrowed more deeply between my thighs, drawing out the elastic surface of my lower belly. I looked at my self, my whole naked self, in the bathroom mirror, frozen in a stubborn silence. I didn't cry. I still think about it now. I think about it very often.

What will I be like when I'm twenty-five? What will my life be like? I was alone and I just sat there on the floor in the darkness as the night closed in. In my sad little notebooks, I would write about the immensity of it all. Where did it start?

I felt as if I were in the corridors of a runaway train as it snaked through the air, I was losing my balance. I tried to carry on walking, grasping onto the taut, brittle threads of a life that was itself hurtling ahead, indifferent. There was some kind of equilibrium to be found, I saw it as a line that was at once short and infinite. It was only then that I could picture time and my own goal, a tiny black speck on the face of this infinity.

There must be some meaning to all of this. I try to stick the pieces together, I can't get them in the right order, there isn't a right order, it just happens as it pleases. And stays.

I had a dream: I'm in a theatre which has been painted in light, pastel colours. There are blue birds, climbing roses and a watery sun. What was once a dirty dusty old theatre is now elegant, airy with plenty of room to circulate. There are young people sitting in corners smoking. I wander around, not really knowing where I am. Too much space for me, too much nothingness. They're all getting ready for something, I get the impression it's some play that defies description – but I know that it has a serious title and that the author lived in a previous century. Then things get confused. I put on the wrong costume, a dark one, and I have a different script to everyone else. I've come to act in another play. Everyone's annoyed with me for getting it wrong. And I can't go back on it, I've signed the contract. I have to pretend, to play the part of the whore (also painted in pastel shades) in the midst of this troupe of jokers who slam doors and caricature their roles like in Feydeau's plays. The theatre is so bright and so clean that there isn't anywhere for me to hide. It all seems so easy and so normal. I made a mistake, I'm the only one who knew and who knew that I was right.

I died.

I feel as if everything about me is wrong. What happened was just the logical extension of a life that was already taken on by others, a group of others to which I still belong. That was where I was born; that's what I've seen and heard; that's how you say it, how you do it, with people like us, and that's what life is like, just like any other. Now I choose, I opt for something, there's no compunction. It's no one's fault but my own. And if I make a mistake, how will I be punished? If I make a mistake, because I pretended to be someone else, but I reveal myself, I reject the trick that I've played by coming back – just for a moment, a lapse in concentration – to my deepest purest self?

It was almost the perfect crime, then just a trace, a suspicion . . . and everything was lost: I died because I made a mistake.

4

In the end I stay at home, losing track of time, just letting it wash over me in its own sweet way. I read, I smoke, I even forget to empty the dirty ash-trays, cultivating my smoker's guilt complex. And the afternoon falls asleep like the dogs lying full-length beside me. It's not long before it's nine o'clock. The youngest, scruffy and sandy-coloured, comes and nuzzles the top of my thigh, slipping his head under the arm of the chair, asking to be stroked. The little fat one lies snoring, perfectly black, perfectly spherical, his smooth coat like a layer of wet rubber, waiting until he's called. I call him quite loudly so that he hears me – he's a little deaf. We cross the busy road together to get to the pedestrian street opposite where we can wander at our leisure, glimpsing people's lives through the eye-level windows. It's a quiet street, the street in which Racine died. It's long and narrow like an alley, and I've never seen it as it is this evening, so long, as long as perfect calm. It's springtime in the dogs' favourite road.

Dogs on leads strain against their collars to wake up their owners who walk along slowly, dreamily. A short little woman goes past with a tall, much younger man. I can hear the unpleasant sound of her heels clicking on the smooth paving stones right to the end of the road, I can hear her vulgar footsteps and her pointless conversation with the tall man beside her.

I like to think as I walk, and I also like to walk. Along the way, I let my mind wander freely. The dogs are free too. This is their allocated time, they busy around endlessly, checking landmarks, completing little circuits, coming and going, organising their canine world. They have manias, they keep repeating themselves but each time is as if it were the first. I love them, I'm gratified by their trust, I gratify them in turn with a pat, and we go home.

Each new day lets you think that spring has arrived. The hardened skin of winter is gradually sloughed off. The shops smell of polish, a big pink magnolia exhales the fragrance of its blooms warmed in the evening breeze. One of the roads opposite rises up a hill, channelling the wind which leaves parcels of sweet smells in its wake. I put my nose into them and close my eyes.

Night falls quickly. Soon you reach that time when you know there's nothing more to do, when time itself has run out, closing its eyes like a light going out. You have to leave the day behind.

And yet this day will count. Like a shadow painted under an eye, its very presence tells a story. But is it the painter's story or the subject's?

The silence was getting thicker every day, ponderously closing our mouths, forcing us to hold back our words. To carry on our lives barely brushing past each other, to forget that we had been alive, heavy. To move us between the abstract vapours of another reality, a reality which knew how to defend itself with words that inevitably lied, in a place where lying is the absolute rule.

A game of wits where the number of probabilities increases with each sentence, each word; a gigantic, infinite multiplication of combinations. A dangerous existence where the spectre of an imaginary world becomes two separate beings, confusing the man with the hero, a unique duo, a disturbing flux between the I and the Him. And for the only one who escapes there's the sorcerer's alcoholic trance, and then the sorcerer becomes sicker than the sick, becomes the warrior and the idiot, and dances the miracle of healing, with his feet on the hot coals and his head swimming in a stupor. A virtual world, a world in which the images conjured by the mind are infinitely demented and evasive.

Chasing the impossible, drawn on by the demon of seductive intelligence which never allows itself to be caught. And you're left with just a few blond hairs between your fingers, instantly knitting with each other, forming letter after letter, entwined, spidery, so minute that you need thousands of them woven together to see the complete picture, as delicate as floating gauze painted the colour of flesh.

A world of illusion where all you do is pretend. But the illusion belongs only to its creator. It sacrifices the world of the living, they die in its gradual accumulation of days and nights, days and nights. It tangles with our living, real-world dreams and clings to our faces that we no longer look at in the mirror because mirrors only show a superficial reflection for those who believe only what they see. The illusion is always beautiful and lets us believe we are immortal. Who invented this illusion, God or the Devil?

Do we have to die, and to make others die, for the angels of this unreal world?

We stopped looking at each other. I didn't want to see that bleary look in his eyes.

5

I would look at something else, anything else, as I crossed the park at Palais-Royal and walked past the children in their rowing boats, the parents with their feet in the sand, the shrivelled little old women quaking in their overgrown shoes, and the lonely in their sober navy blue. They all walked towards me and I would confront them, walking boldly into the sun with my nose in the air. My big, enveloping coat gave me confidence, and my chestnut hair glowed gold.

It could have been the most beautiful moment of my life, it was a beautiful day, and I was pretty that day too. But I would never perform at the Comédie-Française: I had turned down the role of Amélie. I was frequently offered stupid parts, stupid little tarts or just tarts, full-stop, but I didn't feel happy in them. I felt too much compassion for the characters I played. I was born to die for love, not to make fun of it. It was just another director – another man, then – who didn't realise that I could have died like Juliet, like Eurydice, that the actress that I was could become like a child again, a blank sheet, a pure concentrate of love, a creature far stronger and more courageous than the woman that I was.

*

I looked after the parts that I played, but not my life. I felt inside out, like a discarded sock. In the evenings when I undressed the honest woman, I would then put on my bundle of contradictions, slide into the lie; I would put on my old jeans, the ones which made me feel the most comfortable.

I no longer believed that I had to go on inventing rules for myself in true life, in my life, which anyway was no longer my own but had somehow become other people's lives. Why had it escaped my grasp? I let the thread of my story slip away. And I no longer had any illusions. 'How can everything change suddenly, how can you lose yourself somewhere between strength and weakness within your own body?' asked Valéry.

I was going back up the rue de Rivoli, with the Tuileries gardens flitting by on my left. The sky was clouding over, making Paris – the city of lovers – look old and weary. The trees that I glimpsed between the park's iron railings were cut up into a series of vertical slices and seemed to be multiplied into a kaleidoscopic forest. The sky ran like a watercolour in the rain, the colours seeping down to melt and bleach the tree trunks below so that their black surfaces, which had glowed gold in the summer, now veered to peacock blue like splashes of petrol forming circles of yellow and green on the tarmac, in contradictory combinations of colours. The clouds merged together in a range of indistinguishable greys while the ground, scoured by the blades of rain, spewed a palette of natural, earthy sienna pigments, formed channels of saffron and yellow, and stained shoes and stones with splattered blood. The people in the streets bent over as if to wring themselves out. The women with their knees exposed to the weather walked like geishas with their arms crossed under their breasts, holding themselves together round the ribs, lowering their heads and taking quick little steps. Where the rain had pricked the nylon tights on their legs they itched and stung as if a whole stem of nettles had been rubbed against the skin. Their hair stuck to their faces and was held back by fumbling slippery hands.

It was a common spectacle; I knew the street, I didn't know these people but I might as well have done. I often see people that I've seen before, and I recognise them straight away. Paris is the same. So are the seasons.

The Place de la Concorde was very busy; I had the choice between going along the Quais by the river to save time, or up the Champs Elysées to see the cinemas. I had a meeting with a director at one o'clock in a brasserie at the bottom of the Avenue George-V. I chose the Champs Elysées to look at the posters and the faces on the posters. I didn't recognise anyone, nothing was ever the same from one week to the next. I was disappointed by how tawdry the avenue was: the enticing entrances to the cinemas; the dark doorways, glittering with diamanté, where the dancing-girls from the Lido invite you to go in to watch, where no one ever comes out again; fake golden brioches; fake golden shoes; new steel street lights and new beige pavements commissioned by the Paris city council.

In other parts of the city, they're knocking down, evacuating, buying up and building office blocks which will stand empty for those who already have a future ahead of them. In Paris you have to be rich and live in the right *quartiers*. The curved shells of the newspaper kiosks are all pasted with the same slogans, the same people, the ones who have succeeded. They're photographed in front of their houses with their mistresses, their dogs, their jewels,

37

their cars, and their porcelain smiles. They don't have a life, they have money.

I was tired out after spending less than two hours talking to this director. His coffee came at last. To speed up the paying of the bill, I invented another meeting on the other side of Paris, concluding the exhausting meeting with far too much gratitude and enthusiasm. I accumulated words in one last effort not unrelated to the hope of finishing with it as soon as possible, but I felt the discussion setting off again. He picked up the chocolate from his saucer and offered it to me. The tone of the conversation was changing gear, become as sickly-sweet as the chocolate. To me he seemed oily, vain – and stupid. He had a mouth full of words, he was trying to seduce me. I watched his hand stirring his coffee while he watched me, it was a small, spiteful hand and it stuck sweatily to the little spoon. I told myself he was ill, sweating all the time. I brought my head to rest on my hand, slumping my mouth into a little moue of boredom mingled with abandon; I amused myself brushing the tips of my eyelashes with the ends of my fingers and feeling the curve of my cheek with the crook of my hand.

Then I looked straight at him. I didn't slouch forwards – that might have looked to him like a sign of capitulation whereas I'd spent the whole meal trying to make him understand that I could see right through him. That I already understood his film, his life, whether or not he could fuck, whether he was kind or not. I knew I wouldn't be in his film. Whatever emotional, intellectual or human reasons could I have found to do it? I wanted to live every night, every day, a whole year, a whole lifetime enthusiastically, to be inhabited by God, praying for Him not to leave me. What was motivating *him*? His script was useless because he was useless, he couldn't help that, but he obviously didn't realise it. It ended at last. I came back from the cattle market where I'd had to display myself. I felt humiliated, even though I'd done nothing more than listen to him. He hadn't tried to find out about me, that didn't matter to him. The last look he gave me was the worst bit of all. A mayonnaise of pretension and oily simplicity, like the goodbye that he delivered above his head, leaning forwards and waving his spiteful little hand. He bent over as he walked, his shoulders rolled forwards under his black rabbit-fur coat. Even from a distance, there was something perverse about his shoes.

6

First there is the light, white hands crying in the silence, words venturing out, a rasping breath moaning towards life, towards death. I moisten their mouths, leap inside their bellies, I disturb them. Then, as the rain streams from the red-edged sky, the enormity of it is like an echo of nothingness. 'The rest is silence,' Hamlet says as he dies. I would like to act until the day of my death. The curtain falls.

My dressing-room is clammy, like life itself. The lights go out one after another. The costumes gape guilelessly, they look like hanged bodies in the dust, the mirrors are tired. I take some flowers out of their water and they drip onto my clothes; with its make-up off, my face seems thinner. I'm going to let her sleep, and I close the door without a sound. She's lying full-length on the sofa, sleeping in her costume as the white queen. Her translucid pallor is beautiful. Her body is still quivering, shifting like the four layers of a hologram. I can only just make out the outline of her arm and her neck, twitching like the distant twinkle of the stars in the black waters of the sea. Each shivering movement seems to sparkle, like shards of glass shimmering in milk. She was and she will be again tomorrow, nothing can harm her. She has suffered but her lips still smile slightly.

I let go of the door handle, escape into the night. With my little peaked cap on my head, I flee. I should cry because there's nothing left that's mine, I'm leaving empty-handed, empty-hearted too. I carry straight on without looking, I cross the stage from stage left to stage right, like a full-stop, an underlining, all substance has been sucked away – and it's suffocating me. In the coolness of the street outside I feel more relaxed, I feel like staying outside. It is a clear blue night, people are waiting for autographs, I eclipse myself under my hat, I avoid them.

I didn't play my part well. He told me so in the little Italian restaurant across the road from the theatre. The low tables gleamed white, the glasses sparkled and the silver cutlery shone in the empty restaurant. When we came into this pale warmth, red from the cold air in the street, we'd come and sit at this table, between the covered terrace and the more confined interior, between the night outside – the darkness at midnight which I had come to know so well that I no longer noticed it – and the artificial light inside.

I sat down in silence, heavily, with cold hands. I waited for him to talk. He was warm, his shirt was creased, he was looking down, away, trying to understand and leaving me in suspense. I wanted to hear bells clanging together, I wanted to scream, to yell, to tear my arms out, to bite them and tear the flesh, I wanted it to be terrible. I imagined the worst, I hoped for the worst. Let him be wrong, let the night become day, let it be another day in another time, 14 December 1645 for example, let him be someone else, let me not be me. I was prepared to regret everything I'd done so long as I could be forgiven. But I couldn't.

What had happened? He tried, but couldn't understand

who I had become. I could put out my hand to him, to call him all I liked, he could no longer hear me, I was no longer there. He told me I didn't play my part well, that he didn't understand why, and – because I didn't want to explain myself – I knew that he was right, that everything was right . . . except me. My face was puffy and swollen from holding back the truth for too long, my throat was dry, the skin on my throat felt old and stretched and ready to crack, I was white with shame and fear when I came face to face with the worst thing that could happen to me: to be no good. I knew he was telling the truth and that there was some truth to be told. It is a terrible thing when it appears like this, as heavy as the blade of a guillotine, slicing cleanly, precisely.

My spaghetti went cold on the wet plate next to the wet napkin, and my whole soul was drenched in horror. Everything that was left to me, everything that was mine . . . I had managed to tarnish and ruin.

Because every evening I arrived at the theatre at six o'clock. In the deserted bar which led directly onto a long-abandoned balcony, a silent young man was sitting in the gentle light of the end of a summer afternoon. We stayed there together while the others arrived. We'd never ar-ranged to meet, we didn't know each other, but he waited for me and every evening I would arrive early. I wanted him to think I was pretty. I showed off my arms and lifted my hair off the nape of my neck. I liked my hair to tumble gracefully, leaving a few blond wisps here and there to bewitch him. Sometimes he would come and sit down next to me and read a newspaper, spreading it over the square table. We sat elbow to elbow, barely touching each other. I didn't imagine anything further – this closeness was enough, filling me with cold sweat – a kiss in the crook of my neck, perhaps. The empty theatre protected us, and the silence was swallowed up in the velvet. We hid behind the seats, we whispered, like two happy children, the world was ours. Until he became my lover.

He would accompany me all the way back to my dressing-room, which was bathed in light, glowing like an orange-flavoured acid drop. I would get myself ready, put my make-up on, disguise myself. In one of my pockets I had some half-eaten liquorice laces which were like witch's hair. In the other yellow, passion-fruit-flavoured vitamin tablets. I was ready, I would set off to strut up and down the stage, in my clumpy shoes that were tattered, broken and too big for my feet; weighed down by successive layers of skirts and ragged lace petticoats which dragged along the floor in shreds. I would wander about like a clown, walking backwards and forwards grinding the floorboards with the rusted nails on the soles of my shoes. He was leaning against one of the columns in the set, watching me chew a liquorice stick as I twirled and showed off for him. The stage-manager cut across the stage in his rubber-soled trainers. Quite silently he made his way to the console for the electrics on stage; sticking his mouth right up to the microphone he bade good evening to the dressing-rooms on the other floors, and warned that the performance would begin in half an hour. Some of the actors hadn't even arrived yet; but we were already there, in this little air-lock, this little half-hour of our own.

I stretched my legs out in front of me and flexed my feet, then lay stretched out full-length on the floor to ease my back, which was hurting, and I rolled on the ground, perfectly relaxed in my crumpled petticoats – I couldn't care less, my costume was meant to be dirty. I brushed past his leg and sat myself back up again. He hadn't moved and

44

was still watching me sharply. Once again I could feel that he wanted something to happen. I gently fingered the vitamins inside the pocket of my woollen cardigan. I wanted to have one, just to do something, to do something about it, so that he could see me put it in my mouth, so that his eyes followed it into my mouth. I wanted to eat that vitamin tablet, for it to dissolve in my mouth, for my saliva to run in his throat. His eyes followed the movement and asked. I handed him half of it, the sweet clamped between my teeth, my lips parted waiting for his. Let him come and break half of it off in an enforced kiss . . . pushing his share of it with a little prod of my tongue, I felt the inside of his upper lip, and that tiny pinprick of moist contact filled my whole body with honey.

The effect was consumed like a will-o'-the-wisp which disappears instantly, the orange flavour woke me up, I opened my eyes and I saw him looking at me, sucking his portion of the pill.

I made a square with my fingers in front of my eyes so that I could only see part of the picture. Camera zoom in on the naked young woman climbing out of the bath, and she metamorphoses into an old woman. Indecently thin and with sagging flesh and a toothless smile, she grabs hold of the man. I looked for the remote-control, pressed the stop button and walked across the apartment to the bedroom.

I walked through the rooms as if I were drunk, following the contours of the cluttered walls. I didn't notice anything – I didn't know or care about the inquisitive insistence of the heavy pieces of furniture carving into the pitch-dark night. I neither wanted to listen to them nor to recognise their legitimacy. They were there because

I wanted them to be and they were useful to me. I didn't switch on any light, it annoyed me, it was false. I preferred switching it off and coping on my own without taking any advice from goody-two-shoes who always knew how to behave.

The objects in the room contradicted me, tried gently and – in some cases – violently to tell me to pull myself together, leapt at my throat in a final gesture of love, deployed their arms and their charms to tell me to stop, not to go any further. I didn't want to listen to them. I refused to hear their words, I'd always thought they were mute. All these flowers, all these paintings, these armchairs, these vases, this plant that trails all along the wall, these caring maternal tables in tears as they watch me, this friendly carpet slipping under my feet – they were all crying out, rebelling against a silence that had become intolerable. I felt them climbing up to my head and my throat. Even my heart took great slow breaths, tried to restore calm, but failed. It was not sure that I was right and it gradually gave up, impotent, disappointed too, probably. I was making my way towards the last friendly room which generously offered me a mirror, sending back my huge, smooth – human – reflection. Then they all fell silent, they had seen. Their wooden whisperings, their sculptured shoulders, their glass feet no longer had anything to say. I stood naked, looking in the mirror, and I couldn't see anything either, nothing more than some soft, innocent lines, the tilt of a shoulder, the 'S' of a hip, the curve of a little breast like a small toy. There was nothing dirty about it, it was all simplicity without any complications.

It was not what they'd thought.

*

I can hear myself breathing, my face is wet, covered in mucus and tears. My breath shudders like a panting dog. My whole body succumbs to this asphyxiation, I only have a few minutes left to live and yet I am awake, conscious. I can see the pillow swollen with water from my tears, but I can no longer move. I'm lying flat out, naked and hard as a block of wood. I must get it out, but tears and screams are not enough, the pain is too big, too slow to move. It stretches me, toys with me, I screw my whole body up round the exacerbated, atrophied nerve which runs from my head to my feet. My leg rises up of its own accord. I want to scream to God! and to die in myself, to die in myself. I open my eyes, I can still see the pillow, and the pale pink of the sheet. I breath haltingly somewhere between haziness and darkness. I want to snuff out this life that eats away at me, to commit a murder, my own. My body hurts, and when he takes me he lances the abscess. It's the pain that climaxes in an explosive cramp, and the liquid flows like white pus.

Lying there, naked, uncovered, at last ready to die serene and abandoned. I don't want to go to sleep for fear that my dreams will continue to threaten me and that my insomnia will be like my dreams. I don't want to be alone any more, I'm frightened of having too strong a will to die and that this God that I implore will turn out to be a traitor, making me cry out his name only to lose me in its echo.

I was a dead soul, he was alive, young, there was nothing dead about him. I understood that, for the first time, I had come so close to the shadows that even when I was awake I fell into them.

I had to leave, to move to another apartment.

7

I could go on a long journey. Or I could isolate myself, go to the country, up there, in the hills and walk, write and think. But everything changes when the Monday morning telephone begins to ring. The tide of business and things to do excludes all thoughts of distancing oneself, you have to stay where the telephone rings, you have to carve up every hour of your diary into meetings, to talk about all the uncertainties of the future in vague approximative words, and to wait as you wait for a game, for chance, for each pawn to find its place. That's how things fall into place in the greatest game of chance there is.

So I'm going to go to the United States to see whether that's where my important meeting might be. My agent can't see anything wrong with that and even seems relieved to see me going and busying myself somewhere else. Perhaps I'll come back rich and famous.

Just by announcing my departure for Hollywood I've created more of a stir and been met with more enthusiasm than if I were returning with a signed contract from Paramount for a title role opposite Robert De Niro. I leave feeling that I've got nothing to lose. And indeed I lost nothing and gained nothing, except for the rather pathetic respect of those who think I'm over-ambitious. I had to go a very long way to understand once and for all that there's nothing I can do to change the course of events.

But there I was. There's my luggage coming through and I tremble with fear while the American customs men search my bag – shiny shoes, guns and regulation clothes worn slightly undone and sloppy, making them look somehow unwholesome. The cowboy looks at me, I must be guilty then, guilty of having a bag and of being in that airport. They watch strangers coming and going and call over the strangest amongst them. With a flick of their fingers they accuse and discriminate amongst these human specimens buckling under the weight of their luggage, reduced to this vestige of property like tramps who have no other homeland than their bags of belongings. It's like a prison through which you have to pass before you are spat out into the town. First they accuse you, then they set you free, drenched with fear, insecurity and guilt. I'd like to look at my photo albums, to stroke my dogs, and to put a little dried flower at my favourite Buddha's feet, to put on my slippers and cook a meal. And just to make them understand that I'm honest, to tell them about myself so that they understand I'm not as bad as all that. I'm frightened, I know that I'll always be frightened anywhere other than home. I left too quickly.

I got it into my head to travel, and my impatience hurtled me into all these forms of transport. Now, sleepy and dehydrated, I find myself alone in the blue Californian night. Evening falls by seven o'clock. Strange shapes etch themselves across the sweeping hills on either side of the freeway: huge birds plunging their iron beaks into the ground and swinging backwards and forwards without a moment's hesitation. The air is orange-coloured, the sky turquoise – nothing can be confused with anything else here, everything is clear, well defined, simplified. The town stretches before me, flat as a body of water. The roads are black and perfectly straight, perpendicular, criss-crossing like prison bars. Hardly any passers-by pass, not one even. Great expanses lit up by the street-lights and rows of houses, one next to the other.

The man I'm staying with, a friend of a friend, is waiting for me.

It felt as if it was later – darkness can be deceptive. When I get into the house it's only eight o'clock, he's getting ready to go out to dinner. He smells fresh and showered with his wet hair and his after-shave which is still too strong. He takes my bags and looks at me kindly, opens his house and his heart to me, as if we'd known each other for twenty years.

His house is simple, or should I say not complicated. Comfortable rooms with big sofas, a billiard table, a well-equipped kitchen, bedrooms with their own bathrooms, tidy organised cupboards. Outside there's a terrace and a swimming-pool. There are two garages with their throats gaping open at the top of a little rise. My room is below, between the kitchen and the living-room.

In the huge fridge there are new things in unfamiliar packaging. I have to read the label on each pot to know what it is but, for now, I make do with some cheese and a glass of Californian white.

The night hasn't changed, the tone of the darkness has remained the same the whole time. It flows into the valley like a long, weary furrow. The stars multiply and, as I watch them, the night turns white. The houses link together over the brow of the hill. We are on the heights, balancing over the city.

*

I've got a phone number for my American agent – and two or three others, people I don't know, harvested at random from various Parisian contacts. The first is her office number with an extension number along with the first names of her two secretaries. Underneath, written by hand, his home number – just the number. No address.

With my sunglasses and my flowery skirt, I've nothing to fear. I quickly realise that I'm not fashionable and somehow humdrum-looking in my convertible hire car. Whatever: I've got it and it goes! It's hot, the palm trees and lawns are beautiful, the houses clean. In the gardens spiralling shafts of rain splatter the luxuriant flowers with microscopic droplets. As I pass by, my forehead is moistened with a daily veil of dew. I reach the Four Seasons hotel and turn left, moving away from the plants and the shadows, turning my back on them, to confront the hard mass of concrete, harsher than the sky around it. In the heat these great white blocks like pats of butter taken from the fridge transform into a vapour of sand. Nature no longer exists here, everything is straight, obsessive. I go into this kingdom of sand and gold, slipping on the skating rink smoothness of the pavings. I plough on, weighed down by the clogged, burning air, so thick that the sound of the engine is muffled to silence.

I hear her voice before I see her. She speaks loudly but clearly, without giving the impression of shouting. The syllables are each as precise as the directions along a well-known route. Giving an unusual extra weight and length to each word. The strident, insistent music of her monologue betrays no trace of emotion. She's waiting for me: a hot cup of tea is steaming on the low table. It's a large, light room like an interiors shop, Santa Fe style. The half-closed blinds let in the necessary light in a series of stripes. There are pretty piles of paperwork on her desk, earthenware pots holding rulers and pencils, and some flowers. It is these objects who first see me coming into their home, altering the dynamics of their space and, as I take a deep breath, establishing a new configuration of atoms. A second breath, my whole epidermis is on the defensive, I feel nervous and too tall, standing like this in the middle of the room. An unknown place. A first meeting. English. My creased skirt. I look tired. I've put too much make-up on.

I end up asking for a cup of tea that I don't want, and sitting on the sofa I don't feel like sitting on. I know the tea won't be good, and will definitely be too hot. Anyway, the cups aren't even real tea cups, porcelain ones, as they should be, designed so that the opening of the mouth induces equal quantities of saliva to be swallowed with the tea. She herself quietly knocks back litres of Coca-Cola. Litres of it arranged by the dozen in her fridge and in her office. Later, at her house, I would see the same stocks. Hard to conceal my horror in the face of so many units of sugar swallowed at once, these great glasses of liquid caramel quaffed so readily, her throat wide open.

She invites me to stay with her for as long as I like. Hotels are expensive, she must be thinking. I tell her that I'm already staying with a friend, well, the friend of a friend. I don't know him very well, and I don't see much of him but he seems nice. She understands and reiterates her invitation for me to stay with her, if I'd like to. I thank her. There are photographs of children in her office, but I guess that she doesn't have any. I imagine her at home as she is here in her office – alone. With her secretaries, her car, her dogs, her house. But alone in that house, with photographs of other people's children. I also understand why she'd like to persuade me to stay with her, to bring a bit of disorder into her life. I would do this willingly for her as I would to please anyone. We don't say any more about it for today – she'll ask me again another time.

It's still early, and everything is miles from everything else here. All around me there are huge avenues, wide open space, vast parking lots in front of big restaurants, service stations and hotels. I go right down Fairfax to the Farmers' Market to drink some kind of juice. Strawberry, carrot, raspberry, lemon, tomato, cocoa, banana, green bean with a plate of cottage cheese and two slices of pineapple. Then I go back up Sunset and look for the road that leads back up towards the house, which I'm still not very good at locating. I find it and entertain myself dancing in the sunlight round the sweeping corners.

My friend's friend is there, in the kitchen. With his orange and beige bathrobe rolled neatly like a poster round his waist, he's drinking a cup of coffee and eating sweet pastries. I couldn't love a man who eats sweet things in the morning like that. He is alone, sitting down with his back slouched, dunking the pastry in his coffee. I'd been told that his wife had just left him, I wouldn't have thought of him as having a wife. He keeps commenting on the fact that lots of vases have disappeared, or rather that she took them with her. Does she sell vases? Because why would you take vases when you're leaving someone? But I don't say anything. I think what really annoys him about it is that there are spaces, now, where the vases were. So he thinks about these vases while he's eating, bent over the kitchen table.

*

I'd arranged to go and improve my English in a top-flight school. I'd been to the same organisation in London, Paris – and now in LA. In London I'd read Zola; now I don't read, I'm just learning English. I'll have intensive lessons in the morning and for part of the afternoon – six hours of lessons, six tutors a day. But first of all the director of the school, who's been told that I'm coming to study there, invites me to her office to welcome me officially, apparently flattered to know that I'm an actress and that I come with recommendations. She says that my English is fair but has room for improvement. After just ten minutes she knows enough to issue a few orders and draw together the necessary tutors.

I'm going to spend two and a half weeks, and six hours a day in this place. And for two and a half weeks I'll stay at my friend's house, I'll meet a whole load of people, follow complicated itineraries, have a few dinners out in company, at the house, at my agent's house, and I'll go to a few parties.

That's two and a half weeks of going to bed and having the same dream and waking to the same day.

The Venezuelan director has come back at last, and she wants to see me. She's expecting me at two o'clock.

We met for dinner once in Paris. She was ill and had a terrible fever. It was in a pretentious restaurant recommended to me by a 'friend with good taste', a press officer to a number of influential chefs, famous restaurants and prestigious champagne houses. She organised dinners for presidents, and it was her job to keep the presidential menus secret. I'd bumped into her that evening: she was having dinner with her mother, they were at the table by the door in the restaurant – and they were the only clients there. There were no windows, not one – by choice, apparently. The absurd papered the walls. Without a word, without any feeling of conviction, the director and I went in, caught in the trap.

The South American was fairly pretty with a little air of importance that suited her well. She used the sort of American pseudonym typical of off-Broadway jazz singers. I found it difficult to decipher her expression or to hold her eye, not because it was naïve but because it was somehow too huge, and it was accentuated that day by the pallor of her still youthful face. She was a woman of about thirty-nine, she was slim and she obviously took care of herself. Her short-cropped hair left bare the robust nape of her neck, betraying an overly masculine maturity. She had strong, heavy arms, and a thick jaw and neck. Her whole body seemed firm as if it were held in a corset. She had been directing films in Venezuela for a long time. Some of her films had been considered subversive and had been banned by the government. Others – a television series about the national hero, Simon Bolivar – had been very successful and popular. But she had become more ambitious, she had emigrated, found an American husband – the director of one of the biggest film agencies, including mine – and had launched herself on to the heights of Sunset Boulevard, determined and at the ready. Her latest screenplay was more of a fiction than her previous work: it told the story of a love triangle with a girl in the middle. The girl was me. A young girl from a nice family who was proving to be bright and intelligent, torn between two men, both dark, handsome and intelligent themselves – that was how she saw them – two men to love and protect her. This was set against a background of repression and political and emotional intrigue. In short, it was the love-child of *The Famous Five* and *Gone With the Wind*.

56

We both ordered the same ravioli, and drank water while the chef contorted himself into endless simperings. The arrival of each dish, which took as long to come as its name in the menu was pompous, was preceded by this little fanfare. The results were pitiful: dotted here and there on the dry-looking tomato sauce were a few sticky pieces of ravioli, with a little leaf of God knows what to the right and a second leaf of God knows what else on the left. I begged my guest to forgive me for having dragged her into this restaurant, but at least we both shared the slight feeling of having got something wrong, which brought us closer for the first time.

The squirling design of the tomato sauce predicted that I wouldn't be in her film even though I'd gone to Los Angeles in the first place to prepare for the filming: to have the English lessons, lose my excess pounds and meet the people I'd be working with. But the latter changed all the time, like the producers. The film was put off for a few years, eventually made on a shoestring budget – and it still hasn't been released.

I see her regularly now that I'm in LA, and I never enjoy it. She's polite but impenetrable. It could be out of a sense of propriety. I never know, for example, whether or not she's wearing tights. And why does she seem to take such particular care to speak and to dress in a way that lurches from appalling bad taste to the height of refinement? She makes me feel uncomfortable, I don't speak to her; we are camouflaged and cautious with each other.

When she tells me about her film, it's still the same: I understand everything she's saying but I know that she isn't saying everything. I suspect that what she doesn't say disguises a lack of talent, and I can already see myself appearing in a terrible, schmaltzy film, a B-grade series, a garish vulgar airport novel like the horrible abstract and mystical paintings that you find in galleries tucked away in little villages and run by women with cats who smell of patchouli. She watches me at her leisure. It embarrasses me, it's what I hate more than anything, as if the time she takes over each pause between her sentences equated to another hour spent with her. It's always at times like this that I dream of escaping, of her saying that she's got to go to another meeting or that I'm the one who needs to go. Or just that she stops looking at me. I remember that interminable day spent in the sauna. I was a little over-weight and, of course, she'd noticed it. It was only after-wards, as we were going home in her car that she said she'd noticed there were a few extra pounds that needed to go. Always that gratingly gentle tone to give a friendly – but definitive – order.

I think she likes my strong will. With each successive test, I respond where others fail. It matters to me that I don't disappoint her. I'm under her influence, she's stronger than me, but one day I'll find the flaw. We say goodbye to each other in the light that filters from windows of the hotel in which we'd agreed to meet that morning. After the grape-fruit massage at the hands of the Korean girls, and the cold showers, I left her, a shadow sitting. There she was with her short hair and that reserve peculiar to a woman waiting alone in a hotel lounge. But sure of herself all the same, not showing any sign of feeling out of place. She's got into the habit of not liking the world, of defying it. She compares her reality to the reality of others, and thinks that her life weighs heavier than theirs. So she goes about seducing the world in her own suave way, and says nothing. I can imagine her strong, muscly legs rubbing together, hugged by her thick cotton skirt, her back held upright as if by a

58

ruler, and her shoulders – rather thin but gently curving – holding her head upright.

The reception hall yawns between us, I can't hear myself walking on the grey carpet, it's as if I weren't there, I can't hear myself breathing either.

She disappears into the blue background.

I'm going to go back home up the hill on foot. I'm not going to go to bed late, I'll nibble on something I find in the fridge. I just know that nothing will happen.

Mum rang this evening, which reminded me that I hadn't called her. I tell her everything's fine, that the weather's lovely the whole time. She can tell I'm bored but doesn't ask anything, for fear of not understanding, of being clumsy. I just tell her it's a funny kind of life here, that the people are different. I can feel the enormity of the ocean that lies between us. She, with her telephone on the little sideboard in the hall, it's not that cheerful either when I come to think of it, but it's so familiar, it's my whole childhood. The kitchen smelt of soup or fruit tart, and my father's cigarettes when I came home from school. I was seven and I knew he was at home when I saw the white curls of the Gitanes floating in the darkness behind the window. And there's Mum's soft skin, the softest skin. I remember her touch – the absence brings back the memory. There's just been one thing, just the one since my birth. My mother, and her voice talking to me. I'm projected into the person by whom I was made.

An echo of Turgenev:

O youth! youth! you go your way heedless, uncaring – as if you owned all the treasures of the world; even grief elates

59

you, even sorrow sits well upon your brow. You are self-confident and insolent and you say, 'I alone am alive – behold!' even while your own days fly past and vanish without a trace and without number . . .

8

No one's waiting for me at the airport. I've got used to coping on my own, finding my way to the machines to pay for my parking, going down into the subterranean depths, looking for the correct letter at the end of the aisle and gratefully dumping my great shapeless bags. I do it all quickly, with the fluency of someone who does it frequently.

I go home, I'm in my own space and I don't even think about the States any more. It's still morning, I've been travelling through the night. I decided to go to sleep without eating, with just a bottle of mineral water which I filled up again when it was empty. It wasn't a comfortable night, but I feel good, refreshed despite everything and ready to tackle this Parisian day.

I arrive into the pool of morning light drenching the sitting-room of the apartment, and I can hear Mrs H in the kitchen with the dogs. She addresses them by name and carries on an absent-minded conversation with them. Almost before I've opened it the dogs are already obstructing the narrow doorway with their squirming bodies while I try to squeeze through with my cumbersome bags. I see them coming over, ready to growl and bark at whoever might dare to invade their territory, only to begin contorting themselves like slugs as they swing their whole lower bodies from left to right, burying their noses in my bags, and jumping up at my trousers. They look up and open their mouths to reveal their pretty, pearly teeth which emphasise the dark, humid outline of their muzzles, and letting their tongues loll like fine slices of saveloy.

I tussle them and kiss the tops of their heads, holding tightly onto their firm ears. Mrs H comes to greet me in her flowery skirt. We give each other the traditional three kisses, and she, in the confusion, gives me a fourth.

That's all there is waiting for me here, except for the pile of mail heaped on the desk. I sort through it, separating the hand-written letters from those addressed in type which put a 'Mrs' before my name. I look round the apartment, room by room; I even close my eyes before opening the door to my bedroom. I find that nothing has changed. I like Mrs H's orderliness, even if I always move a few objects around after she's been because she has a mania for arranging everything to comply with the laws of symmetry. But it smells good, and it's clean. Mrs H is kind, so are the dogs.

Later on, we have lunch. She puts the meal on the table in dishes that she's taken the trouble to warm in the oven beforehand, the cheese is presented on a little cloth embroidered with ducks, the bottle of wine is uncorked and standing on a napkin. She sits down opposite me and waits for me to help myself first. She has to get up frequently because she always forgets something. In the bread basket she's given me the choice between the two sorts of biscotte that I like as well as fresh bread which she's just bought from the bakery downstairs, nipping down the staircase still wearing her Chinese slippers.

It's good to be home again. I slip back into our little ways and habits. The particular way in which you can live with someone who shares in the intimacy of your apartment without actually being a member of the family, someone you love without telling them so, because that would be too intimate, and someone with whom you always have an element of reserve, keeping over-familiarity at a distance. Our ritual good manners bring a smile to each of our faces as we greet each other in the mornings and say goodbye to each other later – have a good evening, see you tomorrow!

Mrs H arrives promptly at nine o'clock every morning – the dogs wouldn't forgive her a moment's delay. They're ready and eager, regulated like little clocks, waiting for the sound of her key in the lock. I can hear it too from my bed, and it's the starting signal for the beginning of a new day. She comes back half an hour later, and the dogs, full of bounce and wag, come and say hello to me as I finish my breakfast. Every day starts like this, the hours are counted, divided. We co-habit freely – two women and two dogs in the same apartment. I'm on my own and so is she. Her husband died in hospital quite recently, he drank too much, she doesn't drink at all. Sad but relieved, she let him go to a God in whom she believes ardently and to whom she kneels to pray every day in the 'Église des pauvres' in les Halles.

God makes her a good person, if slightly vague. She doesn't stop to ask many questions, and doesn't always understand the message in her bed-time reading, the Bible. She imagines the garden of Eden as being little bigger than the average bedroom, and – to her – God looks like her favourite hero, Richard Chamberlain, eternally young and beautiful, like the pictures on the postcards that she picks up in churches and sends north to her beloved children. If you asked her 'What is Evil? Did the omnipotent God create it?', she wouldn't understand the question, and her sad eyes would cloud over with the contradiction. To her Evil is something indeterminate which you forgive and forget.

She believes in miracles and healing stones. That you have to be good and wait for redemption. God can replace anything, a lover, a true love (something that life never gave her), and she's conjured an image of it as false as its image in bad literature. And, anyway, God looks after everything so well! She calls on him every evening in her room before going to bed. After her confession, she gets up feeling lighter, cleansed of her sins. She's done her duty, the duty of discipline and of admission, which washes everything clean.

If I pass her in the street when she's walking the dogs, her eyes gazing vaguely ahead, I have to call her for her to notice me even if we've been walking straight towards each other for a good fifty yards. I sometimes envy her her calm and her distraction, they would spare me a good deal of trouble and a lot of difficult questions. But it's in the crux of these very questions that I get glimpses of God, and that's why my God is not like hers. Which of us is the happier? I don't know. There have been times when we've cried together, worried about each other, but she thinks that there's a Paradise which promises eternal life, she thinks there are white angels and endless blue skies. Whereas I think . . .

I don't know what I think.

9

'I looked as if I were empty-handed. But I was sure of myself, sure of everything, far surer than he was, sure of my life and of this imminent death. Yes, that was all that was left to me. But at least I held to this truth as closely as it held to me. I had been right, and I still was right, I was always right,' says Camus's *étranger* before his execution.

I walk through the streets and watch the other lonely people walking. There aren't many people around, but enough for it to be obvious that the flow of individuals is increasing. Not one is identical to any of the others. They pass by like a series of images, weightlessly, and yet each of them watches their step along the pavement. Heads bobbing past in the street. My car is parked a little further up, I need to carry on walking, and I like it. Mrs H has gone off into her daydreams again.

As I walk I try to put one foot in front of the other as models are taught to, just in case someone behind me is watching. I want to walk gracefully, upright. Women with curlers bunched round their heads are put on public display through the windows of hairdressing salons. They're concealed from head to foot by their gowns, making them shapeless and ugly, caught *in flagrante delicto* having their beauty treatments. I look away to avoid embarrassing them any further.

It doesn't bother me either way, I never go to the hairdresser. My hairdresser is a friend of mine and we take it in turns to meet at each other's apartments for lunch, for a chat and a laugh, or for him to do my hair for a party, a photo session, or to cut it when it needs it. He wears the same perfume as—

Time stands still and so do I. How should I put it? Him? The man who? The one who? No, it's too much a part of me. He isn't an 'other', outside myself. I can feel him right down to my fingertips, like a glove filled by my hand. His skin covers every inch of me.

I won't nuzzle my nose up to his ear any more, or rub my cheek against his. He's seen me with someone else, my nose against another skin. He tore up the photos, those splashes of meaning on pieces of paper, and left.

The memory has an arrogant tenacity, it clings to me, hurts me, for a split second while I kiss my friend.

Life soldiers on alone at the moment. Like a film set mounted on casters, it trundles past with the same street corners, the same squares, the same churches, the same parks. The well-oiled mechanism runs perfectly smoothly, I don't have to do anything any more, all I can do is regret handing over the relay of my life.

It was a few years ago. We often used to walk along here and dream of living in the Saint-Germain area. Like we used to dream of Italy, a house built of local stone up on the hill, an island lost in the Pacific, an old mechanical printing press to publish new books, dogs, cars by the dozen, a donkey, an orchard – a life full of life. Slowly and contentedly we would gaze through the shop windows and dream: a piece of lace, a chair, a stool, a Venetian light, an unsigned pastel, a pear-wood wardrobe, a tribal amulet, a book of dance cards in a tattered mother-of-pearl case, everything had its own place, its own meaning, life didn't exist without us.

We discovered a little shop crushed under the massive weight of the building above it, which still had the conceit to display a selection of peculiar objects against the deep red velvet of its window dressing. The golden sheen of an old diving mask or a compass was like a hidden treasure discovered in the darkness of a cave bathed in an uncharted blue lagoon. It was 'Red Rackham's treasure'. A model of a three-masted sailing boat in an aquarium was perched on a stand draped in velvet, surrounded by compasses and set-squares.

Men, who invented calculations and discovered the cycles of the moon and the tides, wanted to conquer new lands, draw up maps, build ships and wage wars in order to appropriate the universe.

None of this is particularly evocative for me, except for conjuring the elegant image of a tall, loyal naval officer, like a hero from a book by Conrad. Men with fair eyes and fragile minds, naïve loners striving for some unobtainable ideal, drinking whisky and dreaming of fishing. Good, solid feet, hardly a penny in their pockets – just enough to go and have a drink and talk to the landlord on a dead afternoon in a deserted village.

I came across men like these in my new books and I thought they were better than us, better than women. I admired their simplicity, their openness. By loving them, I myself became more capable of constancy and a sincere sense of wonderment. I would have liked to be like them, to be someone remarkable, to have that beguiling air of distraction – a badly tied shoelace, a wayward tuft of hair not brought into line – and the youthful courage to want to reshape the world, setting sail for years on end, heading as far away as the eye could see, confident that one day they would reach the horizon.

They all dream of discovering America, electricity, the vaccination against tuberculosis, the law of gravity; of being Spinoza, Einstein and Buddha at the same time. If you told them that they had to go right back to the beginning, they would set off with just a small pack on their backs, like the Magician or the Fool – either conscious of their folly or oblivious to it. They wouldn't hesitate for a moment before setting off on the adventure of the world all over again. Their only enemy would be death! One day you have to die and the game is over. Has any of it actually meant anything? Is death the same for everyone, do trees die, does the sea die? Even light fades and dies, so what's left then? Thought, the soul, an endlessly repeated feeling of work left undone, a world chasing its own tail, a world that never ends, spinning on itself. Everything is there, the future exists already. So the castles will crumble only to be built up again and so on *ad infinitum*. Death is always there, it beats even faster than life which is just man's heavy physical counterweight, synthesising illusions and giving form to them. But death, eternity, duality, the perpetual movement by which we measure Time . . . that is what we are. 'Death is the Messiah. That's the real truth,' said Singer.

Full stop. Let's start everything over again. Together. With four feet, four hands, an improbable face uniting life and death, the indispensable and the useless, the possible and the impossible. A continuous, eternal balance.

Did I hear someone say, 'He wants you for his next life?'

I think I did.

10

Bang! I cross over to the other side. I land on my feet at last. Facing the right way, light hearted, and with a clear mind, I make my way forwards – blinded and warmed by it – towards the light. It feels as good as walking along a beach, white feet in smooth sand, gently crushed by the sun's round belly. Like my own rounded belly. And my thighs and breasts. He touched them without even waiting when we kissed for the first time. I let him.

Then he didn't want to see me any more, or even to talk to me, he'd been told all about me. I didn't know anything about him. I thought he was good-looking, with a gentle face, fair complexion and long, tall limbs. He came from somewhere else, spoke another language which I didn't understand, and knew everything about me. We were going to love each other for a long time.

Before, during, after. Far ahead I can see a carpet of heavy fields crushed by a sky that stretches beyond the contours of my eye. Blue, green, black. My pupils dilate, I breathe, I've come back to live in the country. My head is a sphere like the earth itself, and as I was as a child.

I have no luggage, the house is empty, big, white. It's dark, we're alone, he and I. The night is alone too; a beating drum, the echo of hearts beating in the emptiness. We wander around together and look at each other. And the silence rises up, blades of steel brushing past our heads and piercing us. The empty space sharpens our senses, our heads feel alert, raw; our bodies tired and absent. The night is deaf. I can feel the sky coming to rest on my shoulders, catching hold of me and lifting me in a great white ball of air, the grain of sand has passed, it falls, the moment is broken.

Winter, withdrawing from the world, purification, work and sleep. The trees stand jagged in the cold, frozen with terror. The obstinate wind switching allegiances, leaving its mark, the force of nature. Enduring the cold, walking through the stormy weather and coming back refreshed and windswept. The will to live, to have weight, to fight against something bigger than yourself. Like crushing the earth with your own bare feet, ignoring the rain, reshaping the world to suit yourself.

The calm of winter, the arrogance of winter. An ending which never actually dies, a spit in the eye to death. Winter is sarcastic, blessed with happiness.

Those quiet evenings when the dogs sleep with their noses resting on their paws, and we read. Sitting in the warmth reading Singer by the fire, or looking at black and white photographs of a long-lost world, mounted on watercolour paper.

It only takes a breath of wind or even nothing at all, because everything is already there. The same view for years and years. The grass has parted as if by a comb through well-brushed hair. I zig-zag between the young cherry trees and the crumbling mounds of earth made by the stubborn moles, my scarves getting caught on the gossiping thorns of a dog-rose. They want to know every-thing. They hold me back, wait for me to tell them a secret while I untie the knot of threads held in their clutches. I escape and run down our little garden path, I told them I was happy. That's all they wanted to know, and they swing back to let me go.

11

The house no longer exists. One second elapsed, an eternity. The trees are still in blossom and we're leaving. A dog has disappeared. The rooms are empty, the walls too. I leave weighed down, filled up with what was, what has been. Us, our work, our life. And now I'm alone with my lie, and I long to be somewhere else. He leaves alone too, without knowing it. And he dies slowly in the relentless onslaught of depression. He gave everything to his pages of writing, his whole life, it's as simple as that.

It's a lovely day. Behind us the house breathes very quietly so as not to hurt us. A needle in our hearts, we leave it there, with our secrets. Two years, ten years, a hundred years. The pages of a photograph album turning slowly and telling their tale. A whole multitude fixed in one moment, like the sharp point of a diamond tracing the letters of an unknown writing.

Could it be that the gods were here?

I've become a full-time Parisienne again. I'm pale and slim. Energetic, temperamental, talkative, I can't stop saying, doing (though not necessarily doing what I'm saying), moving, moaning, getting up, sitting down, taking deep breaths, settling myself down, finally stopping to catch my breath and sleep. I come and I go, I love cities. I love New York, which I don't yet know; I love Paris, which I know well. So I come and go there as I please, and come back again and again. Then I set off again straight away, driving, driving, and I stop at the Place Vendôme, dazzling white under the sun. I quickly duck into the green and orange tunnels of the deserted ring-road, submerging myself, skimming along, rasping like a long-held breath. I look at the people walking through the streets at Barbès. The fat Arab women with their make-up, their bright colours and their veils, sifting through bundles of linen in the bargain bins outside the shops; and the dusky-skinned men eyeing girls up in the cafés. Everyone is playing a game, the ones who watch and the ones who want to be watched, outside and inside, in the street and on the stage.

That's just the way I look, I just do. Like what? Now, young, happy. Everything's fine, so why worry? A rock song grooving on the radio, a hard peppermint rolling on my tongue, I'm free as the air I breathe. I do whatever comes into my head – or not, as the case may be – and, of course, I'm always right. I'd like to jump three hundred times my own height like a flea, to scream until my lungs tear apart, and then what?

There was no one at the airport, or at the house. The fridge was empty, I daren't even think about the morning, alone – the other side of the bed as stiff as a corpse. What's the point of putting on his slippers and tidying his shoes into the cupboard? What's the point of being here rather than somewhere else, somewhere else rather than here? Dressing up in some disguise to go out, as if I were no longer enough for myself, as if a part of me had left too.

I've run out of weapons and words. I don't want anyone to touch me any more. I'm frightened of being a woman, because I am a woman, there's no doubt about that!

I want to be a queen, and I complain because I'm not Cosette, I want to be intelligent and I don't seem to be capable of it or only when it evades me. I want to smoke cigarettes and to smell nice; really I'd like to be able to be vulgar without anyone realising it. And finally to tell myself that I'll make a fantastic nun – confident that I can do it . . . Final argument against every attack on my femininity which I can forget and repress without any regrets.

But what's wrong with me? Going, but going where? To the cinema? I've already wasted plenty of time like that! To a museum? To have a good conscience, perhaps yes, but also because I like it, I somehow find myself when I look outside. It does me so much good to get out and to think in the light of day, along other lines, in other colours. Celine always moaning, Virginia ranting, Carson – boyish, Proust – gay. But then why not, why not?

I'm feeling better already, I'm back in my cosy home, it smells of untreated wood and lotus incense.

Why isn't he here, at home? All of this is him. This warmth, this décor, much better off than mine steeped in swampy water. It was he who taught me about the world of men. Those who read their newspapers, who collect everything: an article in a magazine, an old Irish tobacco tin, letters from their family, a pebble picked up somewhere, all there on the same shelving unit for twenty years. A world in which nothing is lost, where everything counts, adds up, even a dried flower bud. I like that, and I understand it too. Perhaps I'm a little bit man myself, and that's why I like being gallant with other women, telling them they're pretty and even giving them flowers. From that point of view, I prefer them. They're always cautious, staying on their guard. So much the better.

Actually, I'd do better to go home with my own double but still alone. Or rather I feel like seeing people, doing the rounds of my little world. Where nothing changes?

He's only been my agent for two years. He collects photos too. And what else? I don't know, I don't know him very well. I know he likes boys. What's his apartment like, masculine or feminine?

I often go to see him without warning. So I wait in his secretary's smaller office, she too is new and seems friendly. The poster of the last film she's enjoyed always hangs in pride of place over her head. I sit down opposite her, chat with her while I wait for the meeting next door to finish. I've got all the time in the world. I look at the photos of actors on the walls, they look handsome on the glossy paper, carefully framed like spoilt, beloved children, someone's pride and joy. The picture of me lying full-length, which lives on my agent's bookcase, is languorous and smooth. I'm leaning on my elbows looking serious; but the photograph itself is sophisticated. My face isn't made-up, or looks as if it isn't. There's nothing disturbing about me in it, it's quite a nice picture to have around.

His office is big, I feel comfortable in it. When we're sitting down the distance between us is pleasant, protecting our independence. The chairs are comfortable. We talk to each other with our crossed arms resting on what little space is left on his desk, which is cluttered with piles of white paper toppling precariously like the leaning Tower of Pisa.

He's got a lot to tell me, an unconnected jumble of news, he outlines it briefly and asks me to join him for lunch. He asks me who I met in Los Angeles, he looks intrigued, amused in anticipation. He's there without really being there, he doesn't bother me, or reassure me much either. He listens but at the same time he's following some other train of thought that's come into his head. Alert and absent, he changes the subject, looks out of the window, looks at me with his sky-blue eyes and jumps to something else, dwelling on it for about as long as I will be accorded to tell him what I've been up to.

I might have stayed for ten minutes or an hour, I can never gauge how long we spend together, it always seems both rushed and unhurried. I wait for him to finish a phone call before picking up the thread of a conversation that shifts and changes like the sky galloping overhead.

There are apparently no projects on the horizon. I'm weighed down by a screenplay tucked under my arm, I can't work out how to put my hands in my pockets and to clamp it in position so that it doesn't slip as I walk along. In the end, I just let it go and stop worrying about it. I hesitate. I'd really like to do a feature film, and nothing else, to live in another time, as Kubrik used to say.

Which time do other people live in? What are their lives made of?

My parents are too far away, and we've known each other for too long. For them, I'm the same as I was yesterday, and as I will be tomorrow. It's like sitting in front of the TV, it won't change anything.

I think and I walk on. I could think of all the people I know and let them know. Or go and see a particular girlfriend but I don't know where she is. It's the same, we'd lose each other again in another dimension, the dimension of friendship, stretching out in simple happiness, making no promises. The pavement's annoying me, it's stupid and goes off in every direction. Me too. We're both sulking about each other as I walk along. I don't give a fig for the pavement, the Crazy Horse or any of the rest of it, I haven't even looked at any of it.

I know lots of people who work in this part of Paris. I think of them each in turn, each one calling the next in my mind's eye, for no particular reason. I count them one by one. Each in their own little life, each one original, unique. Making the sum total of all these nothings the all-embracing nothing of loneliness. From a distance I follow their movements in their individual stage sets. Each with their box of colours. More and more into infinity. It's the chain of the world where everything adds up to one, one plus one is one – a strange sum which defies logic. But it's also what we are, what I am. I'm in the chain, unique and just like everyone else.

I get back to the car, which seems to be swelling in the heat of the sun. It'll take me wherever it likes, heading straight for the urban horizon in a brief precise spurt. This machine is far stronger than my state of mind; parading itself, affirming its presence before everything that remains stationary, smacking through the air with a resounding crack.

Grey, blue, pink seen from the bridge. Further on the scenery changes. Under the bridges, under sagging cardboard boxes, lying lifeless at people's feet, people who no longer look like the same species in our tainted eyes. Tainted, maimed, bruised, like rotten meat. Their feet so swollen they're ready to burst, raw, trickling blood. Suffering. Suffering because they no longer have feet to walk. Nothing left at all, then. Absent, with eyes oozing white fluid, and thick pasty tongues, suffocating them silently. The alcoholic vapours melt and fade. They'll disappear, leaving just a pile of ash. I look at them, they're still alive. Surely, it could be me who . . . ? Disfigured bodies still intact, and I'm hurting.

I cross the road to get to a petrol station. I park in front of the pump, just at the foot of the slip-road to the Périphérique. It's hot and dry, there's no one around. I switch off the engine. While I'm taking the keys out of the ignition, I open the door and my stiffened leg comes down onto the ground; I turn round and I see them. Away in the distance, the snaking fumes from the cars make their little silhouettes shimmer, as if they were dancing on tip-toe. I can't make them out very clearly, peering through the smoke to see them. Bang! One of the two bodies rears up out of the clouds and surges into the real world. I suddenly see him, a little boy, wild and agile, he looks as if he's hiding something in his hands. When she comes, he turns towards her. A tall, dark-haired girl, bigger than him. One small step and they set off hand in hand, leaping and jumping over the tarmac from one side of the road to the other. They stop next to the cars, press their noses up to the windows and tilt their heads to ask for coins. I count each stride, my eyes desperate to follow them, trying to understand their game. They slink adroitly between the steaming metal carapaces. He doesn't take his eyes off her. But she plays, play acts, skips, impertinent, and then bounds over to him and lifts him up off the ground because she's bigger than him. They spin round in each other's arms. She puts him down, bends to him, his little arms wrap round her and, with her head on his shoulder, they dance. She kisses his face, his eyelids; hungrily, greedily she covers his face in funny little kisses and holds him to her tightly. They stop moving.

Tiny and black with filth. Drenched with sunlight.

The fuel's overflowing. I take the nozzle out just in time, and hang it back up, it clicks into place, silence . . . Oh yes, I have to pay, the money's in the car, my bag's there with the key in the pocket, I'm not forgetting anything, am I? I can see the till over there, I'm off, I've got everything. The ground underfoot is slightly red, there's a little bank, I go up and over, down to a black fence; now it looks as if there's a passage-way or something over there. How much have I got? A five-franc piece, two two-franc pieces, one note . . . Oh! A gust of wind, my feet are in darkness, it's a bit cold, it's dark, I'm caught in the draft from the passage-way.

She's there, standing stock still in front of me, white skin, dark hair. What's she looking at? She's so pretty, so white, so delicate. I want to see what she's looking at, I can't really make out her eyes in the dark, she runs off, nothing but her colourless little skirt floating like a golden thread eclipsing itself in the darkness.

Chance decided that I should take a different route. Was it by chance? I saw what I wanted to see. Even appearances blur in the dark.

At the theatre one evening a guy came over with an open book and asked me to write what I thought about the purity of feelings. I wrote in capital letters: LOVE.

*

82

It's a long way, and it calms me down, while I think about all this. All this what? It's just all this, isn't it! And what else? Well, him, me, us.

Us, it's good to say us, I feel like several people at once. But maybe that's not all. Part of oneself in a whole body.

He kept looking at me but not speaking. Difficult to say: like knocking at the door that no longer reverberates to the sound. Smothered. The thought of a life without life, exclusion. What should I do, go home? Isolation, there is no home. Go then, go so as not to die again, or die straight away.

I've plenty of time to spare, I know the road well, I leave. Twenty-five. I'm not thinking about dying, for the first time I feel the true weight of things. What do they do in cases like this? Do they follow their own order? Do they coldly apply their laws for killings? Killing one by one or both together? United? But united by what?

By ourselves, a third body.

The chaos, the disorder of fatalities, that is the only god of justice, the only father of truth. He left these two little gypsies to make up their own rules, just so that I could see them up close.

Chance has no previous existence, it's only fulfilled as a result of some fundamental will. It draws on that will before making its appearance, like a clown popping up half-way through a play and shocking the audience. All it is is a moment's pause, an affirmation. The movement continues, everything moves on. Where does needing come from? From the great emptiness which offers up its pearl like an oyster. It imagines a world and then projects it into matter, invents the spirit. It makes everything out of nothingness. Why should there be something instead of nothing? Because there is a need to do something, to raise oneself out of the emptiness, to cry out, to make oneself heard, to be.

To tear one's skin, pinch oneself, beat oneself, to melt into all their arms, gazing up at the sky as they kick the blue emptiness aside. They touch each other as much as they can, gaining weight together as they spin in each other's arms, hurting each other, crashing into each other. I want them to exist, I want to touch them.

Time weighs heavy. In the rear-view mirror I can see that my face has changed. My eyes are buried under my anxious frown. I don't recognise myself with this expression which puts years on me, but it's as if it will be a part of me from now on. The eyes are frightened and the mouth doesn't breathe a word. I know something that I'm not saying. That something appears under the chafed skin, revealing itself. Was it his astringent perfume that dried out the skin on my face and projected me forwards into what I have become? I don't need a mirror any more, I've seen. It's there, on the inside, constantly changing, and visible from the outside, like looking through the windows of the hair-dressing salons.

I turn the steering-wheel as easily as I would a spoon in a bowl of soup, and the car obeys. It skims past the other cars and bends itself round the corners without damaging itself. It surges in response to pressure from my foot, stretching its entire body, letting the blurred images scud past the rear-view mirror.

I was talking to the birds hiding in the laurels. I scratched the trees' legs as I climbed up them, using the sturdy branches to reach the top and sit in their arms. I wasn't afraid of walking barefoot or of sucking the sap from their roots like sucking the tip of an ice-cream cornet, with your head tilted back; I liked nibbling on the black hearts of sunflowers, making the milky sap spring out of wheat germs between my thumb and forefinger, and greedily licking up the sugary white droplets that left a dry floury trail on the hump-back of my tongue.

Like the trails left by aeroplanes in the sky, that life faded away gradually until it was no longer perceptible, until I asked myself whether it had existed at all. We had to sell the house, say how much money, turn away from the blossoming trees parading themselves in their pretty summery prints, and close the garden gate. As if all of it could belong to just anyone, as if you could put the wind in a bag, as if flowers grew to order, as if the birds hiding in the laurels were waiting to be told to go home, as if the sky could carve itself up along the dotted lines of the cadaster. We sold it for money, the dog roses will never forgive me for it, and they continue to sway, chattering to each other, saying I'll never be that happy again.

There are children coming out of school, it's five o'clock already. They're eating huge apple pastries which hide half their faces, and drip apple purée over their grubby un-finished fingers, covered in mud and felt-tip pen. They talk earnestly to their parents, who watch them indulgently. They eat but without thinking about it, their minds on other things. Like walking. Walking like Maxor the Tiger, Maxor who's going to pulverise the planet Hykus with his laser weapon – *Bzing bzing* – and his sword of fire. Maxor is the greatest with his invisibility suit, his all-seeing mask

85

and his radioactive gloves. He sends off his rockets to blow up King Galaxor's planet, *Pow pow vroom vroom vroom*. The children head for home with their heads full of outer space and their satchels full of drawings.

'The smaller they are, the more life they have to live.' They amaze me. Confronted with children I turn into a statue of salt, encrusted in my own sins. Their fragile, supple ability to move and laugh, to tell fantastical stories, makes them as soft as marshmallows, and if they look at me I become consumed in that gaze, as vast as the oceans.

The weather's still nice, and I ask for a pancake from the girl who doesn't know how to make them. She recognises me, and makes it clear that this pancake will be like all the others, just in case I try once again to explain to her how to melt the butter evenly over the batter. She doesn't say anything, neither do I, except that my silence suffers. The pancake won't be nice, and I'll only eat half of it. I throw it in the gutter, frustrated and angry.

If I were her, my pancakes would be the best in Paris.

Mrs H has left. There's a little note on the kitchen table saying she'll see me tomorrow, and a telephone number that I don't recognise. There we go, into the bin. I take my shoes off and put my jacket away in the cupboard. I can hear someone going up the stairs and I look through the spy-hole in the door. I can't make them out clearly in the darkness, and their contours are distorted by the magnifying effect of the glass. They live one floor up, I think. I wouldn't recognise them if I met them in the street, I've only ever seen them in the stairwell, but judging by the way they slop their feet on the stairs, it's them.

Schnitke's requiem is beginning. I still haven't grasped

just how sad it is, sadder than sadness itself. I put on an opera aria instead. The pug's snoring, the other dog's barking at the noisy ghosts in the stairwell until they close their door, and he bounces up and down across the apartment in his tight white trousers, like a ball losing momentum and coming to rest.

More noise on the stairs, and it stops just before the door-bell rings. Now both dogs demonstrate their anger at being disturbed like this at home. Their barking is louder than the music, so I turn off the sound, and go to see who's hiding behind the door. It's the concierge's daughter, one of the twins, I don't know which one, I can't remember their names, anyway. Perhaps they both have the same name? She gives me a big plasticised envelope. 'It's just arrived,' she tells me. She goes back down the stairs as the light goes out. It's from America, the paper is still ice-cold, it must have just come out of the hold of the aeroplane. Inside the plastic bag is the Venezuelan-American film script, still bearing the same title, and the same problems. That makes two screenplays now. I put them away together and pick up a book, resting my stockinged feet on the glass table.

The music is floating on a cushion of air. It breathes in the space around it, and insinuates itself into objects. It invites its way into the most secret states of mind. It stretches out, multiplying itself and disappearing, as fine as lead dust blown by the north wind. It lies down over me, gentle and light. I snuggle down into the feather-light quilt of this substance that has no substance, this non-existent cloud.

What day is it? The telephone won't stop ringing. The washing-machine's churning, and the noises in the street are working themselves into a frenzy. I have to start everything all over again. First I must read the screenplay. Tough decision, and I get it wrong half the time, go back on what I've said, trying to explain my hasty refusal to disappointed producers and directors. I've got to answer the hoards of invitations lying about on my desk, and write cheques for unpaid parking fines. Made out to the Treasury – my treasure. I drink freshly squeezed orange juice to keep me awake until this evening. A friend I haven't seen for ages has invited me out to a little restaurant in Montmartre that I haven't been to before.

12

She always waits for the bell to chime before opening the door. I think she likes to hear it. Mind you, all visitors will already have undergone a preliminary inspection on the intercom before getting to the lifts. But she still waits for her new bell to intone its little ditty before opening up her home. I go in. The television's talking to itself in a corner. The apartment is kept very tidy. It leans into its corners, as if it were limping on its wooden floorboards, or peering to get a better view out of the windows adorned with transparent transfers of roses and lilac blossom. There are neighbours directly opposite, with balconies overlooking the roof-tops of Paris. We're on the top floor. It's pretty. The proximity of the two buildings is the ideal distance for filming from one to the other. Rather like the set in *Rear Window* or in *An American in Paris*, when Gene Kelly wakes up in his room at the beginning of the film. That's how Americans imagine Paris. And that's what Paris is like, too.

She's from the south. From Marseille. She talks loudly because, she says, where she comes from people carry on conversation from one room to the next. Especially the women who busy themselves around the house. She shows me the latest glasses that she picked up at the flea market at seven o'clock one Saturday morning. On the table, a table cloth that she's embroidered with roses.

For twelve years she lived in a studio under the roof. With bathroom, kitchen, bedroom and sitting-room, and the whole thing was probably only twenty-two square metres. Furnished to the nearest centimetre. The bedroom constituted just a bed, like the beds our grandparents used to have, and I would clamber onto it, crushing the eiderdown, delighting in the soft, sensual feeling of well-being in this little doll's bedroom.

Through the sitting-room window brimming with sunlight, great heavy armfuls of heat fell into the room while she cooked her celebrated grilled peppers and sang opera arias with cheeky, street-urchin gusto. She could sing, and she acted in films and for television. When things were difficult she would sell suspender belts that she made herself, asking five hundred francs apiece. Occasionally she would go and work in the restaurant where we were going to eat this evening.

I say she should take off the purple mascara round her eyes. It looks vulgar, especially with green eyes and red hair like hers, with white skin and a double D cup.

She takes me to her restaurant, she drives, scorching off in a cacophony of rattles. I put my bag on my knee and do up my seat belt to please her because she always puts hers on, just as she fills in her tax return, knows a bargain when she sees one, reads legal advice and learns by heart her rights as a consumer, as an employee, as salaried staff and as a home-owner . . . She knows how to save when she has money – when she works, that is. Two months filming in Venezuela, a TV series, a short film, three days for a cameo role, a few extra days, post-synchronising work, she counts everything, takes out a mortgage on ten years of anticipated work, and buys herself a new apartment. She knows everything about overdrawn accounts, repayments, clever shopping when you spend a little but buy a lot, and the little jobs that keep you alive. Months without anything, or just one badly paid day's filming for a commercial, shows that are heading for disaster and will never reach the stage, films running into problems – or at last a part in a prestigious film, with four days' filming: one in May, one in June, one in July and one in August.

She's a good actress, she can play anything, because she's simple and proud. She's played shrews, sexy hair-dressers, and once the part of a barmaid in a Russian coaching inn. She was teaching the ways of love to a young monk who'd escaped from a monastery, singing a tune from an opera, half naked with her big round white breasts which a drunken soldier was sucking at the beginning of the scene. When the stupid actor – who was probably as drunk as his character – acted out the scene he took hold of her breast as he got to his feet, which meant that she had to follow him, attached to this idiot by the breast. She'd had a huge bruise the size of his hand for at least three weeks.

That sort of thing often happened to her. She aroused that urge that some men have to make fun of women, to be dirty and cruel. It could also be said that she was fairly uninhibited in her behaviour, she used crude language and had a loud, abandoned laugh. I've seen her arguing with a biker, throwing insults as if she were a dock-worker from Marseilles, and getting out of her car, pulling up her skirt and pushing up her sleeves. Next to her, I feel tiny, and it's not as if I'm a weakling.

She decided to leave her twenty-two square metres and to get married. She found the husband, undertook the work and paid for the entire wedding as well as the new apartment – all in the twinkling of an eye. A month later I received the solemn piece of white card that was their wedding invitation.

When I visited the future nest of the future husband and wife for the first time, I stopped first in front of the ground-floor windows. The concierge's rabbit had been put there like a china ornament, shut in a cage barely big enough to contain it. It couldn't turn round and just crouched there, unable to use its limbs, paralysed, turning its nose to the opposite wall, frightened and still wild. We stayed with him for a long time, waiting for the man to come back to his little lodge to ask him to set the rabbit free. I told him – I was lying – that I had a house in the country, that it would be very easy to build a run and put the rabbit in it. He needed it, he said, it did him good to have a rabbit. His child liked the rabbit too, and would be heartbroken to lose it. He looked at me, master of his rabbit, master of the window through which we were speaking, master of his choice. He waited for me to stop talking finally and for us to leave. Which we did, rather sadly, leaving the rabbit condemned to its cage, leaving the concierge in his lodge, leaving – also – any hope of being able to change things one day.

Little cherubs danced on the bedroom ceiling, the plinths and door surrounds were painted pale pink, and she had chosen the marble work surface in the kitchen. He still didn't exist, not a single sign of his presence. He was a plumber, apparently, tall and dark, and soon they'd be married. It was written on the white invitation: they'd be married in two weeks' time, at four in the afternoon. She wanted a man in her life, to make love to her, a lot, then a child later. She wanted to hear the noise and hum of a normal life, with its preoccupations – the white wedding, for a start! She was creating her own screenplay, avoiding the awkward questions and the sorry, obvious truth. She couldn't wait for her wedding day.

It never came. The final rush blew itself out. She came to a halt in her hurtling excitement only to realise that she was alone in it. She backtracked and cancelled everything, from the beginning, in the same order.

She wound the film back. The invitations were torn up, the sugared almonds stayed in the kitchen cupboard, the wedding dress still hangs in the wardrobe like an anorexic, the buffet for sixty people was paid for in full. She concluded this episode by moving house again.

She had an accident once on a film shoot – some guy had accidentally twisted her neck when they were dancing. She drove home, her neck giving her blinding headaches. When she got home, she called him. He didn't come, and three days later, when she asked him why, he couldn't give an answer.

She wanted a man, she no longer had one, and she would go on cooking just for herself and her friends.

The rabbit should have made her understand that she'd got the wrong building and the wrong husband, that everyone who lived there was going to die.

The lipstick is a bit much too, but I don't say anything. When I look at the thick paste spread generously over her mouth, applied to exaggerate its contours, I'm overcome by an irresistible desire to rub my own face clean.

I'm tired. I want to move on to something else. A story this time! Beginning, middle and end. As if everything made sense. 'They married and had lots of children.' Why not? It's better than 'She never married and died childless.'

In the end, we all believe more or less in the same things, or perhaps I should say we're all afraid of the same things. So we have children to keep things going. Taking Daddy's name, looking like Mummy (obviously we can't help it), and joining forces with the mystery of life which, for once, is smiling. Then women become extraordinary again, and men become kind. The parents have a second life and are given new meaning in their own children's eyes, children who until then have asked themselves 'Why do Mummy and Daddy look at me like that?' And people come out of hiding all around you to say that they've got little children too, that their lives have changed, that the world has changed. And we dance the round, hand in hand. There's the proof that we don't live for ourselves alone, simpletons dying, bound to die, like old tyres all alone by the side of the road, they will now only ever be useful to some local farmer for holding down the tarpaulin over his stinking silage. Surrounded by other tyres, with their arses in rotting cattle fodder. A lot of trouble for precious little reward.

That's how the Pope will end up, with his arse in the rot, and that also includes all those that he's forced to end up like him, the children who were never quite finished off because their mothers didn't even have the means to get them started. What will he leave behind? A few million victims, and a load of unsold condoms.

And what about me in all this? If I could forget myself a bit, it would give me a break. Come on, I'm waiting for it all to start again and I'm bored to tears.

I'm going to sleep. Just after I close my eyes, absence. The night does its work. On my belly as if on water, I relax snugly into something indefinable. I go to sleep without realising it. Perfectly confident, I dive off into the land of dreams, for eternity. Then it's daytime. A stubborn blade of light dances above my eyelids. Its cutting edge makes an incision into my eye and it flows in.

The day is possible for men of reason, for believers. It is light, for a start.

13

She makes me feel uncomfortable. I can see her there in her suffocating, agitated body, buried in this mass of flesh and knots. Her little black eyes hiding and lying to each other, she no longer looks out but into the uncharted darkness inside. She is pure distress. Her mouth constantly prattling, her hands fidgeting and fiddling the whole time, her pretty face twitching agitatedly into a swarming of incomprehensible and manic grimaces.

She's sitting opposite me, she's eating too much. She fills herself with water, bread, sauces, everything, she fills the void. Her voice rings out shrilly, tensely; her tummy may well be dilated, but her throat is tight.

She makes a lot of noise, knocks things over, bustles into things and people, creating a void around herself. I watch her insistently, and on she goes, bla, bla, bla, she doesn't see me, she never comes out of herself, she can't act, the truth that is herself has worn so thin that she would only have to cut a finger to die in a last spurt of blood. Despite everything, she is brave, takes care of her appearance, keeps her pain to herself. But to achieve this she cannot let time stand still because in that immobility it would reveal her as she is, alone and rootless. She is absent, elusive.

*

He watches her the way people watch fish in an aquarium. He's decided once and for all that it's each for themselves. He comes off better than her, he's content with his life and thinks he's good-looking. He'll always reproach her for letting herself go. He didn't know that he wasn't the one for her. Right now, he can unhitch the chains with which he taught her to follow him.

She will carry on with her frail ankles, her body bent forward, carry on learning the lessons of a life that was never hers.

I took some old photographs of myself from my father's wallet. I didn't know they'd be in there. They're little fragments of life that escape us when we are away from the ones we love. He told me I hadn't changed. I suddenly felt very little, trying to put on the T-shirt in the photo, the T-shirt with the dolphin on it. I can't do it any more, I'm not the same person any more. The contours have changed.

I don't like myself in the past. The life I led then frightens me, I had a narrow escape from it! Danger all around. I'm isolated by that photographed moment, as if the world around me didn't exist. Vampires don't appear on photographs or in mirrors, but the hazy void you see instead is far more disturbing. That void is there on the photo, time stands still now. If I die, it would still be the same photograph . . .

Each memory closes over time, as if time could be cut up into pieces, as if each second had a beginning and an end. Each second can stretch itself and flatten out like an atomic mushroom cloud. I push down hard with my finger. That way I'll live longer, the seconds run on from one to the other and blur together like rings in a pool of water. All you need is one droplet to keep the game going.

I've been on holiday at my parents' house for three weeks. Just a house, and some fields. Nothing and no one else. I feel free. Alone with the sky, the earth, sitting on a slight rise, I watch until I disintegrate and melt completely, my body no longer exists, only my spirit remains, dilating far beyond the world that I see. Below me a young wood, well armed like serried ranks of men with their shields in their fists. It lies motionless and mistrustful, the soft voice of its leaves as they nudge and tickle each other sounds like the lulling whisper of a stream.

One of Valéry's character says: 'I was born in the very place in which I was born to live, but in which I have never lived; a place to which my spirit seems to be transported in an internal journey whenever I'm moved and sad, and weary of life, and enflamed with anger against myself, anger at being someone, and bitten by my very existence which, however pleasant it might be, can turn into sudden and accidental pain. Then I am pierced with the fact of being.'

I still don't have any friends, I'm growing up. I'm ageless, anyway, I've been living for ever. I have a family, a family I've been told is mine. My brother looks like my mother. We have little in common, we don't talk much. It's as if he had a catapult aimed at my face, ready to fire. I pretend to be naïve and I avoid his aim. I think he's unhappy, I've always thought so, we've never told each other the truth.

When I was little, I had a succession of cats and dogs who disappeared one after the other. The cats were born in the cellar but they never stayed. I forced the last one to sleep in my bed with me, I held onto him so that he couldn't escape and when I woke, with scratches on my face, he was no longer there, he'd disappeared in the night.

There were just two little white angels watching over me as I slept.

I travel through time like a tiny grain of sand transported by the wind. I don't know where I come from and I cry a lot. So I come to rest on a leaf which buckles under my weight and I stop moving, I listen. The air is cool and damp. I set off again, flying like a particle of dust. I zig-zag between the trees, and I see fields that I dream of rolling in like a dog without a care in the world, and I see houses that I stop to look over, but I prefer forests, I feel more at home in them, further from people. I roll in the dew, hide in the green moss at the base of tree trunks, and heave myself up to the tops of the powerful oaks. Dazed and intoxicated, I spin round in the spiral up-drafts, rising higher and higher until, quite out of breath, I let myself fall all the way back down onto the sliding backs of the fern fronds, catching all the fresh smells of broken leaves and twigs. Up above, the sky still glides like an idiot.

When night falls again and the exhausted heavy bodies fall silent at last, I take stock. I rummage and snoop. I come right up close to men's fat faces. They're not beautiful. The flies aren't bothered, they amuse themselves crawling ticklingly over them, and I don't recognise anyone. They all look the same, crushed by their own weight. I prefer seeing children asleep.

I have no home, I have no family, I am everywhere and nowhere, it makes no difference to me. Roses are my sisters, dogs my friends.

14

I'm no longer moving, slumped onto the sheets. Only my cheek, on the pillow, seems to have woken up. I think it's Sunday, the bakery's closed today.

I don't want to open my eyes. I let myself melt in this last fraction of time before the last smell and the last breath disappear, by staying motionless I want to cling to the balance of this second which holds my entire life, printed onto its microscopic film. I don't unseal my lips, my tongue stays stuck to my palate, I hold back the moment, lying rigid and tense, I bite it.

The door slams.

My eyes screw up. I try not to suffocate. I stretch and reach out for the door. Behind everything is softness. My nose breaks against the sudden cold, my head cleaves open, I break in two.

The world is still there, soft, insubstantial. I walk sloppily, I'm going to have lunch. I'm not hungry – it's habit, always the same, like the grass-green place mats. His invisible silhouette makes its presence felt too powerfully, I'm the only one breathing here.

He's gone.

This morning he was still asleep here. His leg was asleep, stretched out over the crumpled sheet. His hollow buttock, like a pebble polished by the water, with its soft pearly sheen. The leg flowed precisely, long and elegant, all the way to his foot, a rough-hewn statue. He got up before me to go out. The apartment didn't say a word, it's there spying, sensing, weighing up.

You unplugged something before you left, I can't switch anything on any more.

I chuck out the crumbs from breakfast, I'm going to change, to freshen up and do my hair. I put my boots on, grab a bag, and slam the door. I hold tightly onto the chill banister to stop myself falling. The staircase is crooked, narrow in some places and uneven in others. I count the stairs and forget about them. Seventeen stairs, twenty-three seconds, twenty-four, twenty-five, twenty-seven, two, three, four, seven, four, one, the last two, I jump. A lock of hair breaks loose, my knees tremble. I take a great gulp of air. The door – outlined by its metal casing – throws the blue light at me.

I go out, I don't hear the door closing behind me.

I'm a hell of a liar. I've got lying down to a fine art. Regularly, several times a day, with or without premeditation, spontaneously or brazenly, wide-eyed and sure of myself, I lie.

I'm fleeing from my demons, turning my back on them. I slip away and escape. And yet I transform myself as soon as life picks me up, and then only the truth can be seen. I don't like talking about myself. It's my biggest lie, my best-kept secret.

People tell me that I don't know myself very well. But what is there to know? Every day I breathe millions of new atoms.

Even in the broad light of day, I still wonder who I am.

Those who know me say that I'm serious, pretty and straightforward. The people I work with are happy to have me as an employee in their theatre because they think I'm kind, and fun too. I'm an usherette. Every evening from eight o'clock right through till the interval I'm there in my pink and black uniform, charming and well behaved. Men like to flirt with me. Regularly, several times a day, with or without premeditation, spontaneously or brazenly, wide-eyed and sure of myself, I seduce them.

I've always thought that I was born to act. In the two years that I've been working here, I've seen a lot of actors but I don't like them much.

Alone, in the afternoons, I stand at the top of the dress circle where I allocate the seats, a tiny figure in the red shadows, and I see thousands of lights coming towards me, crackling and breaking on the green of my eyes, wrapping round my neck and ears like a fine piece of silk. I feel comfortable wrapped in it.

Happy, thank God.